"I sure could use a lucky charm."

She frowned. "Lucky charm?"

He nodded. "It was your kiss that brought me good luck."

"Tyler, I hardly think—"

"Hey, don't knock a cowboy for his superstitions," he said, grinning. "So what do you say, care to join me for another night at the rodeo?"

Indecision flickered in her blue eyes.

Tyler's breath caught. He'd be damned, but he almost believed she was tempted. As the male in him considered the possibilities time with Skye might offer, the sensible side of him panicked at the thought of her saying yes. He wasn't looking for an emotional involvement. He had enough problems in his life to deal with already. Tangling with Skye Whitman was one mistake he didn't need to make.

But he knew he would....

Dear Reader,

This April, Silhouette Romance showers you with six spectacular stories from six splendid authors! First, our exciting LOVING THE BOSS miniseries continues as rising star Robin Wells tells the tale of a demure accountant who turns daring to land her boss—and become mommy to *The Executive's Baby*.

Prince Charming's Return signals Myrna Mackenzie's return to Silhouette Romance. In this modern-day fairy-tale romance, wealthy FABULOUS FATHER Gray Alexander discovers he has a son, but the proud mother of his child refuses marriage—unless love enters the equation.... Sandra Steffen's BACHELOR GULCH miniseries is back with *Wes Stryker's Wrangled Wife!* In this spirited story, a pretty stranger just passing through town can't resist a sexy cowboy struggling to raise two orphaned tykes.

Cara Colter revisits the lineup with *Truly Daddy*, an emotional, heartwarming novel about a man who learns what it takes to be a father—and a husband—through the transforming love of a younger woman. When *A Cowboy Comes a Courting* in Christine Scott's contribution to HE'S MY HERO!, the virginal heroine who'd sworn off sexy, stubborn, Stetson-wearing rodeo stars suddenly finds herself falling hopelessly in love. And FAMILY MATTERS showcases Patti Standard's newest novel in which a man with a knack for fixing things sets out to make a struggling single mom and her teenage daughter *His Perfect Family*.

As always, I hope you enjoy this month's offerings, and the wonderful ones still to come!

Happy reading!

Mary-Theresa Hussey

Mary-Theresa Hussey
Senior Editor, Silhouette Romance

Please address questions and book requests to:
Silhouette Reader Service
U.S.: 3010 Walden Ave., P.O. Box 1325, Buffalo, NY 14269
Canadian: P.O. Box 609, Fort Erie, Ont. L2A 5X3

A COWBOY COMES A COURTING

Christine Scott

Silhouette

ROMANCE™

Published by Silhouette Books

America's Publisher of Contemporary Romance

For Joan, Mary Ann and Dorthy,
three wonderful sisters.
Thanks for all your support.

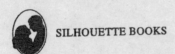 SILHOUETTE BOOKS

ISBN 0-373-19364-5

A COWBOY COMES A COURTING

Copyright © 1999 by Susan Runde

This edition published by arrangement with Harlequin Books S.A.

® and TM are trademarks of Harlequin Books S.A., used under license. Trademarks indicated with ® are registered in the United States Patent and Trademark Office, the Canadian Trade Marks Office and in other countries.

Printed in U.S.A.

Books by Christine Scott

Silhouette Romance

Hazardous Husband #1077
Imitation Bride #1099
Cinderella Bride #1134
I Do? I Don't? #1176
Groom on the Loose #1203
Her Best Man #1321
A Cowboy Comes a Courting #1364

CHRISTINE SCOTT

grew up in Illinois but currently lives in St. Louis, Missouri. A former teacher, she now writes full-time. When she isn't writing romances, she spends her time caring for her husband and three children. In between car pools, baseball games and dance lessons, Christine always finds time to pick up a good book and read about…love. She loves to hear from readers. Write to her at P.O. Box 283, Grover, MO 63040-0283.

Chapter One

"I'm not marrying a cowboy," Skye Whitman announced, raising her chin at a determined angle. "I'm marrying Ralph."

"Now there you go again, jumping to the wrong conclusions." Her father released a disgusted breath. "Did I say you had to marry a cowboy? All I said was, why would you want to go and do a fool, stupid thing like marrying that skinny little, pencil-pushin', four-eyed excuse of a man. For God's sake, girl, Ralph Breedlow can't even hold a decent conversation 'cause he's always got his nose stuck in a book!"

"Ralph's an intellectual," Skye insisted. "He doesn't have time for social niceties."

Lifting a cardboard box from the back of Skye's car, Gus Whitman snorted rudely, giving his opinion on that explanation. "Ralph's a horse's behind. He uses his intelligence as an excuse to be boring."

Skye sighed and grabbed the last box for herself. For the last thirty minutes, she'd been treated to a lecture on the folly of marrying a medieval history professor. She didn't blame her father for being skeptical of Ralph. He wasn't like most men her father knew. As an ex-rodeo star, her father just didn't understand a man who'd never ridden a horse, let alone been near one.

It wasn't Ralph's fault that he didn't fit the cowboy's macho image.

As far as she was concerned, not fitting the cowboy image was what made Ralph so appealing. Though she loved her father dearly, he hadn't always put his family above his true love, the rodeo. If she'd learned anything from her parents' disastrous marriage, it was not to lose her heart to a cowboy.

A trickle of perspiration ran down the valley between her breasts, as she climbed the wooden steps of the family's ranch house. After spending the last six years in the cool, cultured world of the northeast, coming home to the heat and humidity of a Dallas summer to finish her master's thesis in Philosophy was probably not her smartest move. Not only was it as hot as Hades outside, but her father's mood was causing her spirits to wilt fast.

"Gus, could we save this discussion for another day? We haven't seen each other since Christmas. I don't want to waste any of our time together by arguing."

Gus paused at the door to the house, raising a silvering eyebrow in question. "If you don't want to waste any of our time together, then why don't you move into the apartment in Dallas with me?"

Skye's shoulders slumped in defeat. Her father was in one of his cantankerous moods. They both knew he wasn't serious, the offer made out of guilt, rather than the truth. Gus would no more want her to stay with him in the tiny apartment above his Western store in Dallas, than he would want to be forced to live with her at the ranch house that had once belonged to his mother. Either choice involved making a commitment, something her father had never been able to do.

She went along with the game, however, going through the motions of an obligatory refusal. "We've already been through this, Gus. I've been living on my own for a long time. I need my privacy."

"You're not going to get much privacy if you marry Ralph," he pointed out, proving himself to be every bit as stubborn as she'd remembered.

Refusing to be baited into another argument, she let the comment slide without a response. She bumped the front door open with her hip. The house was old, wearing a dusty film of neglect, looking eerily much the same as it had before her grandmother's death six years earlier. "My thesis is very demanding. I'm going to be spending most of my time working. You know as well as I do, you'd never be able to sit by and watch me work without interrupting."

He followed her inside. "I'll be at the store most of the day."

"This is a tough project." She strode into the living room and dropped the box onto the floor, next to an already teetering stack. "I'll be putting in a lot of hours. Day and night."

He scowled. "What's the point of coming home, if you're going to be working all the time? You might as well have stayed up north with *Ralph.*"

"Ralph won't be there," she said without thinking. Giving a silent moan of regret, she averted her gaze. She feigned a sudden interest in a box marked odds and ends, knowing it wouldn't take much for her father to read the disappointment she'd felt at Ralph's decision not to spend the summer with her.

Gus clung to the news like a dog with a bone. "He won't?"

"No, he won't," she said, straightening from the box to face her father. Skye winced at the sudden glint of curiosity in Gus's blue eyes. "He's in Europe for the summer, researching a paper he plans to publish."

"And he didn't take you along?"

"No, he did not." She brushed a dark curl from her forehead, hoping to distract her father. "Whew, it's hot. Would you like a cold drink?"

"Yeah, I'd like a drink," he said, his frown deepening. He pushed the white cowboy hat back from his forehead and scratched at the shock of silver hair, a habit of his when he was trying hard to concentrate. "Since you were knee high to a grasshopper, you've been jabbering away about going to Europe and seeing all those castles that those princes and princesses live in. I can't believe you'd turn down an opportunity to go now."

She strode into the kitchen and pulled two icy bottles of cola from the refrigerator. Twisting the cap on one, she passed it to her father before answering. "Like I said before, I've got a lot of work to do. So does Ralph. I'd have been a distraction—"

"In other words...the idiot didn't ask," her father finished for her, accepting the cola with a grin. Tipping the bottle in salute, he chugged half the soda in one long swallow.

Skye fought the urge to sigh again. She'd done enough sighing for one day, thank you. It was just one of the hazards of being near her father for very long. Leaning against the tiled kitchen counter, sipping her soda, she struggled to find a decorous way to push Gus out the door. "Thanks for helping me move my stuff, Gus. I really appreciate it."

"And now you'd like me to move along, right?"

"Well, I've got a lot of work to do."

"So I've been told," he said wryly. He moved into the living room, eyeing the stacks of boxes, the books scattered about, the computer and software weighing down the dining room table. "Before you put your nose to the grindstone, why don't you play hooky for a night?" He waggled his eyebrows Groucho Marx style. "There's a rodeo in town tonight. And I know some boys that are champing at the bit to see you again."

The "boys" were her father's friends, her adopted "uncles" since she was five years old. It was at this tender age that her mother had died unexpectedly, landing her on her father's doorstep for the duration of her childhood. Divorced for nearly four years and having only seen his daughter a handful of times in between, Gus had been ill-prepared to handle a young girl. At first, he had relied heavily upon the help of his rodeo buddies.

But even with the sage advice of his cohorts, things did not go smoothly. Gus had tried taking her on the road with him. They both soon realized that riding the rodeo circuit wasn't a life for a child, though it was the only life that Gus knew. So he'd placed her at the family ranch in the care of her grandmother. While Grandma Whitman loved her deeply and saw to her needs without complaint, it never quite made up for the abandonment by her only parent.

"Play hooky, eh?" She bit her lip against a smile, trying not to appear too anxious. The truth was, it was just too hot to work. The old house didn't have air conditioning. Until the sun went down, it would remain stifling inside. She'd like nothing more than to escape from the heat and the call of duty for a few more hours. "You always have been a bad influence in my life, Gus."

"I try my best," he said, reaching out to tweak her nose. "You know, honey, you were born too serious. It's my job to see that you have a little fun in your life."

"If you put it that way, how can I say no?" She pushed herself away from the kitchen counter. "Give me a few minutes to find a pair of jeans in this mess. Then you, sir, can escort me to the ball."

With a snort of discontent, the bull pawed the sawdust-strewn ground with his front hooves. Swinging his massive head, he bucked against the gate of the holding pen, ramming the iron fence with a shattering force. His restless movements sent up a cloud of dust and the rank smell of sweaty, raw energy into the air.

Tyler Bradshaw jumped back from the gate, not out of fear, but for safety's sake. In less than an hour, he'd be expected to ride on the back of this restless creature. He didn't need to lose any essential body parts while he was waiting his turn.

Joey Witherspoon chuckled. "Diablo's in a fine mood tonight."

"That he is," Tyler said, his calm voice belying the trepidation churning in his gut. He was getting too old for this. Time to think of retirement. At least, that was what he'd been told by concerned friends.

Not that he felt old. Far from it.

Only, at the age of thirty-two, most bull riders had ended their careers and put themselves out to stud. They'd found themselves pretty little wives and were raising families, settling down to enjoy their retirement while they were still in one piece. But not him, no siree. No primrose path to old age for him.

As far as he was concerned, if he had to hang up his spurs, he might as well be dead.

"How's the back?" Joey asked, studying him carefully. One of his concerned friends, Tyler reminded himself with a sigh. "The back's fine."

"No twinges? No spasms?"

"Not a twitch, not an itch."

Joey didn't crack a smile at his attempt at humor.

Tyler squinted at the man next to him. At an even six feet, they stood eye to eye. But that was where the similarity ended. Joey was dark to Tyler's fair-haired complexion. He was solid-packed muscle to Tyler's lean lankiness. And Joey was a lot smarter than he was. A few years his senior, his friend had had the keen sense to retire years ago from the rodeo circuit. Joey owned a little piece of land not far from Dallas, and he'd found a wife to put up with his pesky ways. Together, they were raising a brood of little Witherspoons. Five, at last count.

"You don't have to ride tonight," Joey said, the words soft enough for Tyler's ears only. "Nobody's going to care if you pass."

"I'm fine, Joey," Tyler said, tight-lipped, reining in his growing irritation.

He didn't need to be reminded of his numerous injuries. A rider worth his salt didn't get to be a champion unless he'd taken a few tumbles. Granted, he did have a tendency to fall on his tailbone, throwing his spinal cord out of whack on more than one occasion. So what if he was becoming a chiropractic junkie, relying on the doctor's magic fingers more and more to work out the kinks? No one ever said the path to glory would be easy.

"Tyler Bradshaw, tell me you're not crazy enough to get on the back of this man-eating bull?" a familiar voice called out.

Tyler grinned, relieved at the interruption. The topic had become entirely too serious for his taste. He turned to welcome the newcomer, Gus Whitman. Tyler owed Gus a great deal. A veteran of the rodeo circuit, the man had taken a raw, seventeen-year-old boy under his wing and coached him to become a champion bull rider. Gus was his mentor, his friend and more of a father figure than Tyler's own pa had ever been.

Pleasure turned to surprise when he spotted his old friend strutting toward him with his arm draped about the shoulders of a beautiful young woman—emphasis on the *young*. Tyler shook his head. Well, he'd be damned. Gus must be feeling his oats tonight—or going through one of those midlife crises—to pick a filly so young.

He raked a second glance over the modern-day Lolita. She had dark—almost black—shiny hair, cut short and framing her oval face. Her big blue eyes were the color of the Texas sky. She had a pert little upturned nose. Her body was petite, but with enough compact curves to make a man sweat. Tyler didn't blame Gus for losing his head over a woman like her, even if she was young enough to be his—

"What's the matter with you, boy? Don't you recognize my daughter?" Gus said, slapping him on the back with a hearty laugh. "It's Skye, you fool."

"Skye?" Tyler repeated dumbly.

It couldn't be. Or could it?

The last time he'd seen Skye Whitman she'd been a flat-chested adolescent, who used to follow him around the rodeo like a lovesick puppy. He'd tolerated her youthful infatuation out of respect for Gus. But he'd kept his distance, never giving her reason to expect more than a brotherly friendship. Back then, she'd been cute enough in a fresh-scrubbed way, but she hadn't looked anything like this grown-up version.

She'd gone away to college a child, and had returned home a woman.

No wonder he hadn't recognized her.

"Hey, Tyler," Skye said, her rosebud lips parting in an easy smile. "It's been a long time."

Even the voice was different, he realized. All rich and sultry, reminding him of the taste of milk chocolate melting in his mouth on a hot, summer day.

Somehow he found his own voice. "Skye, I can't believe it's you."

An understatement for sure.

"It hasn't been that long, has it?" The smooth lines of her forehead puckered into a frown. "Well, I guess it has been a few years. Six, right?"

"Yeah, I guess so," he said, aware that a half-dozen sets of eyes were upon him. They were drawing a small crowd. All of Gus's cronies who still hung about the rodeo were beginning to zero in on their little group.

Unexplainably, Tyler felt a flash of resentment. He'd have liked to have had a moment alone with this new Skye. His gaze flitted over the lush curves of her breasts, the tiny nip of her waist and the gentle splay of her hips. Given a little time, he just might develop an infatuation of his own.

"Skye's home for the summer to work on her thesis," Gus said, his paternal pride showing through. "A regular college degree isn't enough for my little girl, she has to get a master's degree to boot."

Like a slap in the face, the words brought Tyler reeling back to reality. He bridled his prurient thoughts concerning Skye, steering them in a safer direction. Skye Whitman was as off limits to him today as she had been six years ago. She was still Gus's daughter, not a rodeo groupie. He didn't care how grown-up the lady might appear.

Play around with her heart, and he'd be playing with fire.

Tyler Bradshaw hadn't changed a bit.

Well, maybe a little. The squint lines around his eyes were deeper. The planes of his face were a little sharper, a little more rugged. And though he was still lean and lanky, he'd filled out some, appearing more solid. But he was still the heartbreaker she'd always remembered.

One of those cowboys she'd sworn to avoid.

What was different this time, she told herself, was that she'd been on the receiving end of one of those assessing gazes of his. That head-to-toe scrutiny of a discerning eye. Tyler Bradshaw was a man who loved women. The notches on his bedposts certainly attested to that fact. She couldn't deny a certain titillating thrill that, after all these years, she'd finally caught his eye.

Six years ago, she'd have killed to have him notice her. Now, it only made her wary.

"I'm getting married," Skye blurted out.

A stunned silence met her announcement.

Tyler blinked, looking surprised.

Gus scowled, shaking his head in disgust.

"Congratulations, Skye," Joey Witherspoon said, the first to react. "Who's the lucky man?"

"Man?" Gus snorted.

"Ralph Breedlow," Skye said, jumping in before everyone was treated to her father's jaded opinion of her intended. "He's an associate professor at the college I've been attending."

"A *medieval* history professor," Gus added, not hiding his disdain.

"Gus, really," she said. "Now isn't the time to discuss—"

"When's the wedding?" Tyler interrupted, his deep voice sending a chill down her spine.

Skye shifted uneasily from one foot to the other. "Well, we haven't exactly set a date yet."

"Ralph's too busy," Gus explained. "He's in Europe for the summer, reading some dusty old books."

Tyler raised a brow. "And he's left you home all alone?"

"Ralph trusts me," she said, raising her chin.

"You aren't the one Ralph should be worried about." Tyler's easy smile revealed a set of perfect toothpaste-ad teeth. "It's us disappointed men and all our broken hearts that you'll be leaving behind."

Skye felt a flush of discomfort creep up her face. She'd issued the announcement of her pending marriage as a warning to Tyler Bradshaw to keep his distance. Somehow, he'd taken her unavailability as a challenge. He seemed determined to make her admit that she wasn't really serious about Ralph.

"Just as soon as we set a date, I'll be sure to invite you to the wedding," she said, smiling sweetly. "A free meal is the least I can offer you to patch up that broken heart."

A hoot of laughter erupted from the crowd.

"I don't know about a broken heart, but I'd sure like to have my turn at kissing the bride," one of her father's buddies interjected. A tall, thin man, wearing a tan western shirt and black bolero tie, enveloped her in a bone-crushing hug. Bussing her cheek with a fleeting kiss, he murmured, "Congratulations, Skye."

One by one, her "uncles" crowded in to take their turns.

Gus suffered through the mandatory pats on the back and the murmurs of congratulations with his usual good cheer. He shook his head and groused the entire time.

Her own head was reeling by the time the last cowboy stood waiting to collect his kiss.

Tyler Bradshaw watched her with a devilish glint in his eye.

An unexplainable panic gripped her, making it hard to breathe. Frantically, she searched her mind for a plausible excuse for bowing out of the ritual. Unfortunately, she couldn't come up with a single, logical reason why Tyler—though much younger than most of her father's friends—should be denied the friendly kiss while she'd indulged the rest of the group.

As though he sensed her reluctance, a grin played on his tantalizing lips.

Skye's stomach lurched with trepidation.

Over the PA system, participants for the last event of the night were being called to the starting chutes. Skye breathed a quiet sigh of relief as she heard Tyler's name among the bull riders. With a wide smile, she pointed a finger to the invisible voice in the sky. "Someone's calling your name."

"You want me to leave without giving the bride a kiss?"

"Oh, I think I'll survive without the attention."

He stepped toward her.

"I-I don't think there's enough time...." she stammered, fighting the urge to back away. "Besides, it's such a silly tradition, don't you think? Just an excuse for men to take advantage."

"Well now," he drawled, caressing her with a rakish glance. "I'm not sure I can speak for everyone else, but this cowboy's big on tradition. But if you'd rather skip the ritual, that's fine with me." He tapped his whiskery cheek with a long, tapered finger. "Though I'd sure appreciate a little kiss for good luck, before I start my ride."

Skye swallowed hard, glancing around to see if anyone was watching.

The whole crew of cowboys was waiting for her answer. Each of them wore a smile of amusement on his weathered face. Her father wore the biggest grin of all. She could see the laughter dancing in Gus's eyes. Her daddy expected her to tell Tyler no.

"Well, hell," she muttered, releasing an exasperated breath, as she was struck with an ill-advised surge of reckless defiance. "I don't want to be accused of bringing a cowboy bad luck."

She stood on tiptoe, propping both hands on Tyler's shoulders for balance, feeling the heat of his skin and the strength of his muscles through the thin fabric of his western shirt. The touch warmed her hands, warmed her body. Up close, he was all male, hard planes and chiseled angles. Scents mingled—spicy aftershave, rugged leather and hardworking sweat—making her dizzy with the combination. Before second thoughts could stop her, she puckered up to give him an innocent peck on the cheek.

Whether it was an accident, or a well-calculated dastardly act, she would never know. Instead of the chaste kiss she'd meant to give him, Tyler lowered his head and turned just in time to collect a full-mouthed smack on the lips.

For a pint-size woman, Skye packed a kiss with a major league wallop. Soft, warm and supple, her mouth seemed made to fit his. Tyler's lips sizzled at the impact. He felt the shocked inhalation of breath against his mouth. She swayed slightly. Before she could escape, he grabbed a hold of her tiny waist and held on tight.

The kiss, by his standards, was innocent enough. No tongue and cheek action. No plundering of the virginal mouth. Just an innocent pressing of his lips to hers. But the way his blood was heating and his body was thrumming, he'd have thought he was on his way to a blissful night in heaven.

Heaven would have to wait.

He felt the insistent weight of her hands against his shoulders and realized Skye was trying to push him away. Reluctantly, he did as she'd requested. He released the grip he had on her waist, instantly missing the sweet heat of her body as she slipped away.

If they weren't in the middle of a crowded rodeo, fast becoming the center of attention, he'd have pushed for a second helping of this unexpected treat. But he valued his life too much to risk the wrath of Gus Whitman. He'd rather face an ornery bull, than an irate father.

He took a good look at the woman who'd affected him so. Truth be told, Skye looked a little tipsy. There was a dazed, uncertain look clouding those big blue eyes. Her lips parted slightly as she sucked in a deep breath. The action stretched the material of her T-shirt against her generous curves, making his mouth go dry and his body ache with a new awareness.

He reconsidered that second kiss.

But before he gave in to temptation, he had the good sense to look up and catch Gus's eye. His mentor, the man he respected more than anyone else in the world, was watching him with the guarded expression of a hawk about to swoop down and attack.

Giving what he hoped was a nonchalant smile, Tyler

tipped his hat in mock salute. "Thank you, ma'am. If that doesn't bring me a little luck, I don't know what will."

Then, without a backward glance, he strode away, carrying with him the memory of Skye's good-luck kiss.

Until Diablo demanded his full attention.

Moved from the holding pen into the bucking chute, the bull looked raring to trample any fool who dared to climb aboard. That fool being himself, Tyler mused. When his turn was announced, he settled himself onto the bull's back. Tuning out the noise of the arena, he slipped his gloved hand through the handhold, palm upward. Then, once, twice, he wrapped the end of loose rope across his hand, strapping himself to eighteen hundred pounds of molten energy. As he prepared for his ride, the bull's loose hide twitched restlessly beneath him.

Tyler knew that the fury called Diablo was about to be unleashed.

Not wanting to delay the inevitable, Tyler nodded to the gate tender. The gate burst open. Diablo took a fraction of a second to glance around. Then, with a roll of his eyes, the bull arched his back and threw himself sideways out of the chute.

Struggling for balance, Tyler dug in his spurs and tried to center himself on Diablo's back, avoiding the worst of the seesaw bucking action. As the bull rounded for another jump, Tyler squeezed the rope in a death grip, trying his best not to get thrown off. The urge to grab ahold and hang on for dear life nearly overwhelmed him. Somehow, he had the presence of mind to keep his free hand up and out of the way as required.

Like the devil himself, Diablo tried a new method to pull him under. He made a sharp turn to the left and began to spin. The world swirled around him, faster and faster until Tyler felt as though he were about to be sucked into an invisible whirlpool of motion.

Then just as quickly as he began, Diablo stopped his spin. He kicked his heels and began to buck once again. With a snort and a bellow of indignation, the bull tried to toss him off his back. Tyler felt every hop, every bounce, every jolt in his clenched, aching muscles. His spine felt as though it were being rattled apart.

Then, just when he thought he could endure no more, the horn sounded. His eight seconds of hell were over.

Tyler released his grip on the bull rope. With his free hand, he loosened the tight wrap around his riding hand. A final buck sent him flying off the back of the bull. He landed hard, the breath knocked out of him. He lay stunned on his back, wondering if he'd ever be able to move again.

Nearby, Diablo snorted. He lowered his massive head and pawed the dirt, preparing for a final charge.

Tyler forced his aching body to move. Rolling over onto his side, he hopped up and scrambled for the fence.

Two clowns jumped into the line of fire. Running, hollering and whistling, they distracted Diablo long enough for Tyler to make it to safety.

A cheer rose from the arena.

Tyler knew he'd had the best ride of the night. If only his bruised muscles would let him enjoy the moment.

A small group of well-wishers gathered around him. His gaze darted around, seeking the face of the woman he knew he'd be better off forgetting. With a sigh of relief, he spotted her in the crowd. Slowly, he made his way to Skye's side.

"Best ride of the night," she said, sounding only slightly impressed.

He shrugged, resisting the urge to brag. "Yeah, well,

tonight's just the qualifying rounds. Tomorrow's the finals." Leaning his aching weight against the fence for support, he angled a glance at her, his gaze lingering on her full lips. "I guess I couldn't talk you into coming tomorrow night, could I? I sure could use a lucky charm."

She frowned. "Lucky charm?"

He nodded. "It was your kiss that brought me good luck."

"Tyler, I hardly think—"

"Hey, don't knock a cowboy for his superstitions," he said, grinning. "So what do you say, care to join me for another night at the rodeo?"

Indecision flickered in her blue eyes.

Tyler's breath caught. He'd be damned, but he almost believed she was tempted. As the male in him considered the possibilities time with Skye might offer, the sensible side of him panicked at the thought of her saying yes. He wasn't looking for an emotional involvement. He had enough problems in his life to deal with already. Tangling with Gus's daughter was one mistake he didn't need to make.

"Thanks, but no thanks, Tyler," she said finally. "I appreciate the offer, but I've got a lot of things on my mind right now. What with the trip home, cleaning up the ranch house, my thesis—"

"And Ralph," he reminded her.

A tinge of embarrassed color touched her cheeks. "Yes, of course...Ralph, too."

"Just my luck. Find my lucky charm, only to learn it belongs to someone else," he said, with the exaggerated sigh of a man who knew he'd been given a reprieve. He straightened from the fence, flexing his shoulders, trying not to cry out with each painful movement. "Oh, well, I guess I'll just have to tough it out without you."

"Don't worry, Tyler," she said with a shake of her head. "I have a feeling you're the kind of man who can land on his feet...no matter what the circumstances."

Tyler looked at her in surprise and was struck with the uncanny feeling that, with her refusal, he'd been luckier than he'd first thought.

Despite the years they'd been apart, Skye knew him all too well.

Chapter Two

"His lucky charm," Skye muttered, rattling a stack of research papers in her fisted hand. "What does he think I am? A Kewpie doll?"

Silence was her only answer in the empty house. After years of living in the city, she had to reacquaint herself with the quietude of the country. Her nearest neighbor was Jack, an old family friend who managed the ranch and looked after her father's horses. He lived in a small house a few miles from the ranch house. Too far for a pop-in visit whenever she got lonely. It wasn't any wonder that, with nothing else to distract her, her mind wandered to Tyler's unforgettable image.

"Why am I wasting my time thinking about Tyler Bradshaw?" she growled. "I've got work to do."

After a day of unpacking and settling in, she'd had an early dinner then taken a cold shower to cool off. She'd dressed in the most comfortable outfit she could find—a blue tank top and a pair of short white cutoffs—and seated herself at the dining room table to put in a few hours of work on her paper.

The problem was...she couldn't concentrate.

A soft breeze stirred the air, lifting the lace curtains, doing little to relieve the stifling heat. Skye lifted a cube of ice from her iced tea and pressed it against the back of her neck. In all her years of living in Texas, she couldn't remember a summer being quite so hot. She felt as though she were melting from the inside out, like a mushy ice cream bar.

Water from the ice cube dripped onto her research papers, splotching the printed ink with a big, fat drop.

Skye moaned and rose from the table, taking her glass of tea with her. Tossing the ice cube in the kitchen sink, she returned to the living room, plopped herself down onto the frayed chintz couch and picked up the TV's remote control. Mindlessly, she flipped through the meager offering of channels on the tube. Baseball, reruns, news...and the rodeo.

"Switch the channel," she told herself. There was nothing at the rodeo to interest her. Nothing, and no one. She lifted the remote control, her finger poised on the channel button, ready to turn off this spectacle of male machismo, but she couldn't find the strength to do it.

Last night had been the first time in years that she'd been to a rodeo. She'd forgotten how they intrigued her, in a discomforting sort of way. Like a bypasser unable to stop gawking at the scene of an automobile accident, she just couldn't turn away.

While in college, she'd divorced herself from the life her father loved. She'd logically, morally and intellectually convinced herself that cowboys and the rodeo in which they lived exemplified all that was wrong with the world. They were risk takers. They were reckless and vain, so caught up in winning a purse and proving they were the best, that they forgot the families who loved them and were waiting for them at home.

Skye sighed, knowing that the root of her own troubled childhood was showing. That the resentment toward her father and the life he'd chosen over her mother and herself was influencing her judgment. But she couldn't help herself. In her heart, the rodeo and emotional pain would always be irrevocably interwoven.

Which didn't make her sudden interest in the rodeo and, in particular, a certain cowboy any easier to understand.

"Skye, Skye, Skye," she murmured to herself. "You've got enough trouble in your life. Don't go looking for more."

The bull riders were announced.

Skye cursed the grainy screen of her ancient television. After last night, seeing the action firsthand, the fuzzy picture seemed sadly lacking in comparison. Dropping the remote control on the coffee table, she leaned forward in her seat and squinted at the tube.

Tyler was fourth in the lineup. The first rider touched a gloved hand to the bronco's back and was disqualified. The second rider had a decent ride, not perfect, but good enough to put him in the running. By the third rider, Skye shot a nervous glance at the telephone and toyed with the idea of calling Ralph. She dismissed the idea out of hand. Ralph had called late last night. He'd been vague and distant, his mind obviously on the dusty tomes he was researching, not on her. She'd ended the conversation with a curt goodbye, telling him when he was really interested in what she had to say to call her back.

Only, he hadn't.

The thought of calling him now grated on her conscience. It would be tantamount to surrendering her feminine pride. Once and for all, Ralph Breedlow had to learn to appreciate her.

She refused to play second fiddle in any man's life.

"Our fourth rider of the night is veteran bull rider, three-time World Champion, Tyler Bradshaw." A cheer arose from the arena at the announcement.

Riveted to the TV screen, Skye bit her lip as she waited for the bull to burst out of the chute.

"He'll be riding Tornado this evening," the announcer continued. "Hold on to your hats, ladies and gentlemen. This bull likes to dance to the twist."

The gate swung open and the bull carrying Tyler hopped out. It was a thick-bodied, short-legged, mottled Brangus, a bull that was half Brahma, half Angus. Its horns had been lopped off to protect the rider, but its long, square head looked menacing enough to cause damage.

She couldn't see Tyler's face beneath the wide brim of his black cowboy hat. But she recognized the confident set of his wide shoulders, the narrow breadth of his jean-clad hips, and his long, sinewy legs covered in leather chaps. He exuded confidence wrought of experience. He almost made her believe bull riding was as easy as a stroll down the street.

Silently, Skye counted off the seconds in unison with the clock at the bottom of the television screen. Tyler held on with perfect form for the first two seconds. By the third, she knew he was in trouble.

The bull rounded into a sharp circle, looking like a dog chasing his tail. Round and round he spun Tyler, flopping him against his back like a rag doll. Then, he reversed his direction, snapping Tyler off his back and sending him sailing into the air.

Only, Tyler's hand was hooked in the rope's handhold.

Unable to react fast enough, he was dragged across the pen by a bull who looked determined to kill him.

"Ladies and gentlemen, it looks as though Bradshaw's in trouble now," the announcer's voice whined.

"No kidding," Skye hollered at the television.

Rodeo clowns hopped into the ring, trying their best to corner the runaway bull.

Tornado lived up to his name by lurching in the opposite direction, spinning around on his back hooves, his front hooves landing directly on the center of Tyler's stomach.

Her heart thumping, Skye shot to her feet, gasping at the scene being played out on the television.

Another set of rodeo clowns jumped into the arena, rushing headlong into the bull's path. For the next few minutes, she watched in horror as the men worked to subdue the out-of-control bull.

In a blink of an eye, she'd relived her worst childhood nightmare, a cowboy trampled by a bull. Of course, as a child, it had been her father who'd suffered the damage. Knowing it was Tyler, her father's protégé, didn't make it any easier.

After what seemed like an eternity, Tyler was released from his deadly bond with the bull. He lay limp in the sawdust and dirt, before the emergency paramedics whisked him out of the arena.

Skye paced the floor of the living room, half listening to the announcer's account of the incident, cringing when they insisted on replaying each and every gory moment, not once, but twice. No word on Tyler's condition, however.

Releasing a growl of frustration, she strode into the kitchen and snatched up the wall phone. Thanking the advances of modern-day technology, she punched in the number for her father's cell phone.

Gus picked up on the fourth ring. "Gus Whitman," he barked into the phone, skipping the usual polite greeting. He sounded as tense as she felt.

"Gus," she said, unable to stop the quaver in her voice. "I was just watching Tyler's ride."

"Aw, honey." Gus sighed, his tone softening. "I wish you hadn't."

"Is he okay? Have you seen him?"

"Just for a second, before they hauled him away." Gus paused. "He didn't look too good. But what do you expect from somebody who's just been tossed around by a bull?"

Skye twisted the cord of the phone around her fingers, trying to swallow the lump of emotion in her throat. "He got more than tossed, Gus. The bull landed on top of him. Got him dead to rights in the middle of his stomach."

Gus didn't reply right away.

"Talk to me, Gus. How is he?"

"He's awake. But he ain't cussin' like he ought to be." Gus sighed deeply. "I just don't know what to tell ya, honey."

For once, she believed he was telling her the truth. "Where are they taking him?"

"Dallas Memorial. I'm on my way there, as we speak. I'll give you a holler just as soon as I hear anything new. I promise."

He was trying to change his ways, Skye told herself. He really was trying.

"Thanks, Daddy," she said, barely noticing the traditional address. She'd called her father Gus for so many years, she had no idea why she felt the sudden need to address him differently. "I'll be waiting to hear from you."

Slowly, she unwrapped the cocoon of phone wire that she'd woven around her fingers, then returned the receiver to its cradle. Gus was looking after Tyler, she told herself. He wouldn't be alone. That was all that mattered.

A picture of Tyler last night, leaning against the arena fence, looking healthy and flushed with the thrill of victory, flashed through her mind. She recalled the devilish grin on his lips when he'd said, "I guess I couldn't talk you into coming tomorrow night, could I? I sure could use a lucky charm."

She closed her eyes against the memory. Tyler's accident wasn't her responsibility, she told herself. Lucky charms, superstitions and cowboy traditions were all a bunch of bull, no pun intended. Her refusal to attend tonight's performance did not cause Tyler's accident. It was his own stupid fault for riding that crazy bull.

His own stupid fault...

Slowly, she opened her eyes. If the accident wasn't her responsibility, then why did her gut feel as though it had been stomped on right along with Tyler's?

She made her decision quickly, not giving herself a chance to change her mind. Turning off the television, she gathered up her purse and car keys and headed out the door for Dallas Memorial.

"He has a concussion, cracked ribs, a sprained wrist, multiple bruises and lacerations," the doctor said, reading his notes from an open hospital chart. He addressed his comments to Gus, as though Tyler weren't even in the hospital room. "But that isn't the worst of his injuries. At the moment, I'm more concerned about his back."

Tyler closed his eyes, the only movement that didn't

hurt, wishing he could make the two hovering men disappear from his mind as easily as from sight.

"As you know, he's been through this before. I've warned him the spinal cord is delicate. It isn't designed to take this type of repeated abuse. But obviously Mr. Bradshaw didn't hear my advice."

"I heard you. I simply ignored you," Tyler said, opening his eyes. "And would you two mind not talking about me like I'm not here. I'm not dead, am I?"

"No, not yet," the doctor said, shooting him a stern look. "But another stunt like this one and that might be the case."

Tyler drew in a slow breath, wincing as the movement jarred his injured ribs. He didn't need to be told the ride had been a bust from the start; he already knew it. Unable to get a firm seat on the bull from the moment they'd shot out of the chute, he'd spent most of the ride sliding around on Tornado's back. By the time the bull had started his spinning routine, Tyler knew he was a goner.

"I'll be keeping him overnight for observation," the doctor said, glancing at Gus, before turning his attention to Tyler. "We'll discuss your back in the morning. For now, get some rest, Mr. Bradshaw. You're going to need it."

Snapping the chart closed with a click, the doctor spun around on his heel and strode from the room.

"Got a nice bedside manner, doesn't he?" Tyler drawled, watching the man's dramatic exit with a wry glance.

Gus didn't say a word.

Warily, Tyler turned his attention to his friend.

Gus stood at the foot of his bed, his hands on his hips, a forbidding look on his face.

"Now what?" Tyler sighed.

"Sometimes you make me so damned mad—" Gus stopped, blew out a whistling breath. Then, glaring at him, he added, "If you weren't so banged up already, I'd try knocking some sense into that stubborn head of yours."

"Well, thank you, Gus. I appreciate your concern."

Pointing a finger at Tyler's nose, Gus hollered, "This is one situation you can't joke your way out of. I was there the last time you hurt your back. Even if you don't remember the doctor's warning, I do. Your spine's going to snap like a twig one of these days if you don't stop riding those damned bulls."

Tyler stared at him, remaining stubbornly mute.

"What's the matter with you, boy? Don't you understand? The next time a bull decides to use you as a punchin' bag, you won't be walking away from it—if he doesn't kill you first."

The words chilled him. Tyler looked away, not allowing his friend to see his unease. It wasn't that he had a death wish, he told himself. Or that he wanted to spend the rest of his life in a wheelchair. It was just that who he was, what he was, was so tied up with the rodeo, he couldn't separate the two. Not even at the high price he'd be forced to pay.

"You've won every title there is," Gus said. "What more is there to prove?"

That he was Tyler Bradshaw, bull rider, rodeo champion. That he was somebody more than the hick kid who took off from home at the age of seventeen—

"Tyler, listen to me," Gus said, lowering his voice from a roar to a whisper, his tone deadly somber. "You've got to face the facts. It's time to retire."

Unexplainably, his friend's gentle concern irritated Tyler more than his irate preaching. He felt the anger swirl in his stomach, the nonsensical words burn in his mind, knew they were uncalled-for, his animosity ill-advised. But for the life of him, he couldn't stop the angry words from tumbling out. "If and when I retire, it'll be *my* decision. Not yours, old man."

Gus flinched as though he'd been dealt a blow.

All of Tyler's aching body parts combined didn't feel half as bad as the pain in his heart at having hurt his mentor. Tyler owed him his career, his life. He wanted to reach out and apologize, to tell Gus he didn't mean it. Only he didn't know how.

The door to his hospital room opened, saving him from the effort.

Skye stood in the doorway, looking small, pale and frightened. The heavy door whisked shut behind her, causing her to jump in surprise. Her concern on top of Gus's was the last straw.

Tyler scowled. "What is this, a funeral? Sorry, Skye. I'm not dead yet. You're going to have to wait a few months for a visitation."

Unlike her father, who'd taken his abuse with stoic silence, Skye gave him tit for tat. The expression on her face changed dramatically, from scared to stormy. "Tyler Bradshaw, you are the most ungrateful man to walk this planet. Why anybody bothers to care about you is beyond me."

He narrowed a glance at the fireball, unable to curb a grudging admiration for her spunky attitude. She was certainly her father's daughter. Not one to back away from a fight.

Her eyes sparkled as she continued, "But for some crazy reason, they do. Now there's a hall full of cowboys waiting outside. And they're not leaving until they've seen for themselves that you're okay. So just shut up and endure the attention."

With that she opened the hospital room door and peered out into the hall. Motioning with one slender hand, she stepped back and allowed the well-wishers to enter.

Slim, Joey, Bucky, Mark...and more crowded into the room. Tyler hadn't seen this many of the boys since they'd celebrated a rookie's initial ride at the Watering Hole bar. Tyler lay back in his bed and moaned. He almost wished the bull had finished the job he'd started. Even in the best of conditions, Tyler wasn't good at being social, preferring to be an observer, rather than a participant. Tonight, feeling as though he'd been run over by a truck, he just wanted to curl up and feel sorry for himself.

Tyler opened his mouth to bite out a quick dismissal of the group, but thought better of it, when he caught Skye's glowering gaze. He'd be better off taking on Tornado again, than butting heads with her.

Skye Whitman was one woman he didn't want to cross.

From a spot in the corner of the room, away from the center of action, Skye watched the interchange between Tyler and his friends. She'd never met a man who so carefully guarded even the simplest show of emotion. Every time one of the boys brought up his injuries, he changed the subject. If they asked how he felt after his harrowing ride, he brushed it off with a joke. He hid his feelings behind a good ol' boy mask of indifference. Not letting anyone see the real Tyler Bradshaw.

Whoever that might be.

The nurse on duty, a harried young woman with long blond hair and a worried frown, entered the room, pushing her way through the crowd. "Gentlemen, it's after visiting hours. Our patient's tired. He needs his rest. I'm sorry, but ya'll have to leave now."

Murmurs of regret sounded in the room.

The nurse hadn't been the only one to notice Tyler's eyes drifting shut more than once. Or his ashen pallor. Or the grimace of pain that he tried to hide behind a strained smile. Without an argument, the cowboys mumbled their goodbyes and began drifting toward the door.

It was time to go home.

Skye watched the men's slow exodus and wondered if, with the setting sun, the ranch house had cooled down any. Or if it was still sweltering with heat.

She noticed her father deep in conversation with Joey Witherspoon at the foot of Tyler's bed. Their voices were low, hushed in deference to the now sleeping Tyler. Her curiosity piqued, she sidled up to the pair.

"He's going to need help," Gus was telling his friend. "He's got some cracked ribs and he's done a number on his back again. Doctor says he's going to need to rest and recuperate. But, hell, he lives out of that damn truck of his, driving from one rodeo to the next. Where's he supposed to go?"

"Juanita and I would like to help." Joey flexed his massive shoulders into a shrug. "But with the new baby, Juanita already has her hands full."

"My apartment's too small to turn around in, let alone have a houseguest," Gus muttered, glancing at Tyler's still figure. "Dammit, what are we going to do with him?"

"Surely, somebody could take him in."

"Who?" Gus asked sharply. "Don't get me wrong. Tyler's a good ol' boy and all, but—" He sighed. "Well, I don't know too many cowboys fool enough to stay within kickin' distance of him when he's been hurt. He can be a bit on the cantankerous side."

Skye clapped a hand to her mouth, smothering a laugh.

Gus Whitman calling Tyler Bradshaw cantankerous was a little like the pot calling the kettle black.

The noise caught both men's attention.

Joey turned, startled. "Hey there, Skye. I didn't notice you standing there."

Gus frowned. "Honey, I thought you'd left along with the others."

"I just thought I'd stay and see how Tyler's doing," she said, instantly regretting the words. Admitting to her father that she was worried about Tyler didn't seem like a wise thing to do. She shrugged, covering her concern. "You know, to see if he needed anything, like a toothbrush, or a magazine, or something."

The two men exchanged a glance.

Gus cleared his throat and gave his most engaging smile. "Say, honey…how's that ranch house? Gettin' kind of lonely?"

Skye frowned. "Lonely? No, not yet anyway. I mean, it's a lot different from living in the city—" She stopped herself, stared at the two men, seeing the wheels turning behind their guarded expressions. She gave her head a slow, disbelieving shake. "Oh, no, you don't—"

"Don't what, honey?" Gus asked, a picture of innocence.

"Tyler…" she sputtered, waving a hand at the injured man's prone form. "You're not going to foist him off on me to nurse."

The mere thought sent the heat of anger racing through her veins—along with another emotion she didn't want to dwell on at the moment. Her father was certainly running true to form. Once again, he was pushing his obligations off onto another person—namely, herself.

"He's not in that bad a shape," Gus protested weakly. As though on cue, Tyler moaned in his sleep. In sync, they turned their heads to look at him. He looked even paler than before. Deep lines of pain furrowed his brow. The bump on his head was taking on an ugly red hue.

Not that bad a shape, ha!

Skye fastened a hard look on her father, trying a new tack. "Think about this, Gus. We're talking about Tyler Bradshaw, the man who dated three women on the same night in Little Rock. He barely got out of town one step ahead of an irate boyfriend and two bloodthirsty fathers. Do you really want to leave your own daughter alone with this man?"

"Tyler?" Gus thumbed a gesture at his friend. "He's too banged up to do anybody any harm."

Skye growled. "I thought you just said he wasn't in that bad a shape."

Joey watched the exchange in wide-eyed silence, with all the wariness of a man who had two young daughters of his own at home.

"Look, Skye," Gus pleaded. "You'd be doing me a big favor. There isn't anybody else who can help. I wouldn't ask except Tyler's an old friend. He's like a—" Gus stopped himself, then glanced away, his cheeks flushing with color.

Like a son, Skye silently finished for him, experiencing an emotion that felt suspiciously like jealousy. Gus had never kept his feelings for Tyler a secret. Skye had been a mere child when he'd taken Tyler under his wing. She'd watched with an envious eye all the attention her father had showered on the youth, showing him the ropes of bullriding, helping him earn his stripes as a top-seeded rodeo star. Tyler had been his protégé. The light Skye could never hope to compete with in her father's eye.

Appalled by these feelings, unable to admit to anyone—not even herself—that she was resentful of Tyler in any way, Skye gave a defeated sigh. "All right, Gus. If you really want me to help, then I guess it'll be okay if Tyler stays at the ranch with me for a few days."

"The hell I will," a deep voice interrupted them.

Skye jumped, casting a startled glance at the bed. And caught Tyler's stormy gaze.

The patient was awake.

"No way," Tyler said, making his point clear. "I don't need a nursemaid."

Especially not a nursemaid like Skye, he added silently.

"Just how far do you think you're going to get without help, Tyler?" Gus asked, his expression thunderous. "You're as weak as a newborn colt. And just as wobbly, too."

Gus was right, of course. His head was throbbing. He felt each of his cracked ribs every time he drew a breath. The wrist was so sore and swollen, he could barely move his fingers. And his back...each movement brought a new spasm of pain zigzagging up and down his spine. Tyler had no idea how he was going to walk out of this hospital room, let alone cope on his own.

"I'll get by," Tyler said, trying to sound stoic.

"The hell you will," Gus said, shaking his head in frustration. "If it isn't at the ranch with Skye, then we'll have to find you somewhere else to go. What's the harm in spending a few days with Skye?"

Tyler stared at him, wondering if his friend was really that naive. Skye was a beautiful, desirable woman. Wounded or not, any man's willpower would be tested. The problem was, he didn't know how to explain to his mentor the real reason why he didn't trust himself to be alone with her.

"Tyler, listen," Skye said, her tone resigned. "I don't

want a houseguest any more than you want to stay at the ranch with me. But I don't see that we have much of a choice. Granted, it's not going to be easy sharing living quarters. But I'll be working most of the time on my thesis. You'll hardly even know I'm there.''

Tyler cast a surreptitious glance over the tight-fitting tank top and the white cutoffs that hugged her generous curves. He frowned as he studied the smooth length of bare legs. Not noticing Skye would be like trying to ignore a ten-pound powder keg that was about to explode.

Oblivious to his troublesome thoughts, she continued, ''I promise, I'll stay out of your way...unless you need me.''

Need her? Tyler bit back a moan, wondering if a man could be condemned just for the prurient thoughts running through his mind.

''You'll be doing me a favor, really,'' she insisted, forcing a smile. Her rosebud lips parted, revealing a set of even white teeth, and Tyler was instantly reminded of the kiss they'd shared. He licked his lips, his mouth suddenly feeling dry, parched. ''The ranch is kind of lonely. It'll be nice to have someone to keep me company.''

A lie if he'd ever heard one. The problem was, as far as he could see, Skye was forcing him to make the decision. If he turned her down, he'd be the bad guy. If he said yes, there would be hell to pay, for sure.

''So what do you say, Tyler?'' she asked. ''Want to let an old friend help you out?''

Since she'd put it like that, he'd sound like an ungrateful cad if he said no. Lifting his good hand, he rubbed the grit out of his weary eyes and sighed. ''All right, Skye. I'll stay for a couple of days.''

''Great,'' she said, her smile tightening. ''It'll be fun.''

''Fun?'' Gus asked, a vein pulsing at his temple. He

looked as though he were having second thoughts. "Now look, young lady—"

"What's the matter with you, Gus?" Skye asked, laughing off her father's latent streak of paternal protectiveness. "You're the one who suggested he stay with me in the first place. Like you've said a hundred times before, Tyler's like a son to you. Then that must make him like a brother to me. We haven't seen each other for years. It'll be nice to catch up."

A brother? She thought of him as a brother? Tyler scowled. The night was going from bad to worse.

Joey lifted a hand to his mouth, hiding an amused grin, looking as though he were about to bust a gut to keep from laughing. He cleared his throat. "I think I'd better be going."

"Me, too," Skye said. "I've got a lot of things to do before tomorrow." She waggled her fingers in a goodbye salute, then shot Tyler an innocent smile as she followed Joey to the door. "See ya in the morning, Tyler."

"Right," Tyler muttered. "Good night, sis."

Her step faltered. She gave him an uncertain look, then disappeared through the hospital door.

Gus hesitated before following the pair. He narrowed his gaze, looking as unconvinced as Tyler felt at this newfound sibling relationship. "Don't worry about a thing, Tyler. I'll be checking in on you two as often as possible. Just to make sure Skye hasn't taken on anything more than she can handle."

The warning was clearly noted. Touch Gus's daughter and he'd die a slow and painful death.

Gus strode from the room, leaving Tyler alone to stew in silence.

He might have his faults, but stupidity wasn't one of them. Not only was he going to have to suffer through his injuries from the bull, but he was going to have to endure an ungodly amount of torture. He was going to be cared for by a beautiful woman who swore she thought of him only as a brother.

A brother, eh? It would be a hell of a challenge to prove her wrong.

Chapter Three

"Are you aiming for the potholes?" Tyler asked, clenching his teeth against the fresh pain each bump in the ride from the hospital brought him.

Since Skye's arrival at the hospital this morning, he'd been in a foul mood, not his usual cheerful self. He'd been thrown off a bull before, but he'd never felt quite this bad. And that was why he was feeling so ornery and out of sorts.

Or so he told himself.

He refused to admit his tetchy mood might have something to do with the prospect of spending time alone, in close—and all too tempting—confines, with the woman sitting next to him in this pint-size car of hers.

"No, I'm not aiming for the holes," Skye said, frowning. "The road's a nightmare. I have no idea when it was last paved."

"Paved?" He chuckled, glancing outside at the cloud of dust the little car was kicking up. "You have been living in the city too long."

Her scowl deepened. "Tyler, for someone who's being granted a huge favor, you aren't acting very grateful."

"Oh, I'm grateful, Skye." He shifted his bruised tail-bone against the vinyl seat, wishing the aging vehicle had more legroom. Wishing he wasn't forced to sit so close to Skye, so that every time he breathed he inhaled the sweet scent of her perfume. "It isn't every day I'm squeezed into a tin can-size car with a set of broken ribs, a bum wrist and an aching back. Don't worry, though, I get thrown by bulls on a regular basis. I'm used to pain."

"You wanted more room? Too bad I left the Mercedes up north," she said, snapping her fingers, taking his complaints in stride. "Next time I come home to Texas, I'll be sure to bring it along."

He glanced at her sharply, ignoring her sarcasm. "Plan on leaving again soon?"

She took her eyes off the dirt road long enough to look at him in surprise. "This visit's only for the summer. I haven't moved back to Texas for good. Ralph's job is in Boston—"

"Ralph," Tyler interrupted, uncertain why he felt a sudden flash of irritation. "That's the fiancé, right?"

"Right," she said, her brow crinkling into a frown. "He's a professor. Jobs aren't easy to get in the academic field. He has to go where he's wanted."

"I suppose there's not much call for medieval history in Texas," he drawled.

If she noticed the mockery in his tone, she didn't mention it. Instead, she reached a hand to the dashboard and flipped on the windshield wipers, doing her best to clear off the worst of the film of dust that had settled across the window. He noticed the slender fingers on her left hand were ringless.

"So, Ralph's not big on tradition, eh?"

She looked at him again, this time in confusion.

He pointed to her ringless hand. "No diamond."

A tinge of color settled across her cheeks. "Well, the engagement's not exactly official. It's still in the planning stage."

"Planning stage?"

"We're working on the details, ironing out a few of the kinks."

"Kind of like a business deal, hmm?"

She squirmed in her seat and Tyler realized he was enjoying her discomfort way too much.

"There's nothing wrong with approaching marriage in a logical, sensible manner," she said. "The divorce rate in this country is way too high. If more people took the time to think things through, rather than act on emotion and impulse, the courts wouldn't be half as busy dealing with failed marriages."

"Then again," Tyler said, watching her closely, "if more people didn't bother with a wedding in the first place, there wouldn't be a need for divorce court."

A strained silence filled the car. All that he heard was the thumping of the wipers against the windshield and the pounding of his own heart.

"So you don't believe in marriage," she said finally, her tone flat.

"Not for this cowboy," he said, grabbing for a handhold as the car bumped unheedingly across a gaping pothole. Unfortunately, he reached with his sore hand, causing his wrist to pulsate with pain. He bit back a curse. "For Pete's sake, Skye. Slow down. Are you trying to kill me, or what? I don't remember the ranch being this far out of town. It feels like we've been driving forever."

"Be patient, Tyler. We're almost there."

"Yeah, well, I haven't seen a house in ages," he groused.

She shrugged, frowning. "So it's a little isolated."

"A little isolated? This place is practically deserted. Don't you get lonely out here?"

"What is this? An inquisition?" Her frown deepened. "I like being by myself, don't you?"

"Well, sure. But I don't mind giving a few friends the chance to drop by once in a while, either," he said, knowing he didn't give a dang about the isolation. It was the thought of him and Skye alone, with no one else in sight, that had him on edge.

"I saw plenty of people when I was at school up north. It's nice to get away from the stress when I'm home." With a relieved expression, she said, "Speaking of which...here we are, home sweet home."

"Home sweet home" was a faded white clapboard, one-and-a-half-story house. A dismal little building with blue shutters that were weathered and peeling in places. The grounds had a minimal amount of shrubbery and landscaping, giving it a barren appearance. What little grass and bushes there were lay wilting, gasping for water in the hot Texas sun.

"It's...um...nice," he said politely.

"It could be," she said, making him wonder if she'd become a mind reader while attending college. Ignoring his curious gaze, she continued, "Gus doesn't have the heart to sell the family homeplace. But he doesn't have the desire to give it the attention it really needs, either." She raised a brow, glancing at him. "How about you, Tyler. Interested in becoming a rancher?"

"Who, me?" Tyler looked at her, uncertain how much Gus had told her about his injuries. He lifted his wrapped and sore wrist, wincing at the needles of pain. "This is only a temporary setback. I'll be on my feet and back on the rodeo circuit in no time.''

"Of course you will,'' she said, revealing nothing but sincerity in her tone. Her eyes focused straight ahead, however, her gaze trained on the narrow lane leading to the house, making him wonder why she didn't want to face him.

Tyler blew out a pent-up breath. The pain was affecting his judgment. He was becoming paranoid, looking for trouble where there wasn't any to be found. Skye was being supportive, helping him out when he was in need. He had no right to question her motives.

Skye jerked the little car to a stop, parking as close to the front door as possible. Once the dust settled, she opened the car door and stepped outside. With a catlike grace, she stretched her arms above her head, causing her T-shirt to ride up an inch or two, revealing her smooth, flat tummy.

"Goodness.'' She sighed. "It feels great to stretch my legs.''

Pushing aside the erotic thoughts her svelte figure conjured up, Tyler took his time joining her. His raging hormones would have to wait, he told himself. He had a more pressing problem to handle. Earlier at the hospital, with the help of an orderly and a wheelchair, Skye had gotten him into this tiny car of hers. He wasn't sure how she expected to get him out.

Opening the car door seemed to use up all of his energy. Breathing deeply, bracing himself, he swung one leg, then the other onto the ground outside. Then he waited, closing his eyes and clenching his muscles against the rippling tide of pain that washed over his body.

"Let me help,'' Skye said, her voice close.

He opened his eyes and found her standing before him,

her cheeks flushed from the heat, her skin moist with perspiration, her dark hair curling about her face from the humidity. She couldn't be more than five foot three, probably weighed a hundred pounds, soaking wet. How she thought she could lift a hundred and eighty pounds of solid male was beyond him.

"Just give me a second," he said, flushing more with the heat of embarrassment than the heat of the day, the helplessness of his condition hitting home for the first time. "I'll get myself out of here, by and by."

Skye leaned an arm against the open car door, studying him for a long moment. "Tyler, are you going to be this stubborn the entire time you're here? Not that I'm complaining, mind you. It's just I'd like to know in advance, so I can prepare myself for the next time you fall flat on your face."

He glared at her. "You really are a smart alec, aren't you?"

"Guilty." She smiled at his consternation. "What do you say, Tyler? Humor the little lady. Let her give you a hand getting out of her 'tin can' car."

Had he really called her car a 'tin can'? Tyler winced at the reminder. He wouldn't blame her if she drove him to the nearest bus station and sent him back to Dallas. Though he hated to admit it, the thought of leaving her was doing some strange things to his head. He just might miss her smart mouth and pretty face.

"All right," he said, reaching out his uninjured hand. "You pull, while I push. Between the two of us, we just might get this aching body movin'."

Grabbing his arm, Skye flexed her knees and dug the heels of her sandals into the dirt of the road. She looked like a weightlifter, preparing to press a couple of hundred pounds. "On the count of three, Tyler. One, two, three…"

With her yanking on his arm, and him putting as much strength behind a push as he could muster, somehow he wobbled to his feet. It took him a moment to straighten, however. Feeling like an old man, he slowly, carefully, unkinked his back.

Skye heaved a sigh of relief. "Great, now all we have to do is get you into the house."

"I'll be fine." Tyler eyed the stone path leading to the front porch and the wooden steps leading to the door. The distance loomed before him. He slumped his weight against the car, tired from just thinking of the prospect. "Just give me a second to catch my breath."

"Come on, Tyler," she said, draping his arm about her shoulders. "Jack, the ranch manager, bought us a window air conditioner this morning. Set it up in the dining room, so it can cool the whole downstairs of the house. You'll breathe easier in air-conditioning, not out here in the hot sun."

"Are you trying to tempt me, Skye Whitman?" he asked, grimacing as she pressed her soft curves against his bruised ribs, wishing he were in better shape to enjoy the moment.

"I'm trying to get you to move," she said, releasing an exasperated breath. "Come on, Tyler, just one step at a time. That's it. You're doing great."

He bit his tongue, stopping an angry retort at her patronizing tone. The last thing he wanted to do was antagonize a woman who had the power to dump him flat on his butt in the middle of nowhere.

Somehow they made it up the steps to the front door. Breathing heavily, sounding as though they'd run a mile, or, at the very least, spent the last hour making passionate love, they stared at the heavy, carved oak door.

"Got a key, Skye?"

"It's on the doorsill," she said, lifting her chin to point out the location. Keeping one arm secured around his waist, with her free hand she reached above her head, feeling carefully for the hidden key. Finding it, she unlocked the door.

A rush of cool refreshing air wafted over them.

Skye moaned in ecstasy.

Tyler nearly smiled at her delight.

In silent assent, they continued their trek inside.

Skye kicked the door with the heel of her sandal, closing it with a thud. "Let's get you into bed."

At another time, the suggestion might have intrigued him. Today, it only irritated him, making him all the more aware of his limitations. "I've been in bed all morning," he complained, setting his jaw at a stubborn angle. "I just need a place to sit down."

"I still think you'd be better off in bed. You look like you're about ready to drop in your tracks."

"Just help me over to the couch," he muttered, not needing another reminder of his weakened state.

His landing wasn't nearly as smooth as his takeoff. Awkwardly, with Skye hanging on to balance him, he fell across the length of the couch. The momentum of his sudden drop took her by surprise. She landed spread-eagle across his chest. In any other circumstance, he might have enjoyed the situation. But as it was, every inch of his body yelled out in protest at the unexpected weight. He heard a cry of pain, and realized it had come from him.

Skye scrambled to her feet, leaning over him with a concerned look on her face. "Are you okay? Jeez, Tyler, I'm sorry. Did I do any permanent damage?"

Tyler stared at her, too stunned to speak. The pain he could manage. He was used to enduring its tenacious hold. What he wasn't sure he could handle was the view her stooped posture afforded, that and the gaping neckline of her T-shirt.

Feeling like a voyeur, his body responded like any normal red-blooded male who'd been treated to a peek at Skye's décolletage. Blood pumped to his groin, arousing him. While annoyed by his reaction, he was also secretly relieved that at least one essential part of his anatomy hadn't been damaged by the trampling bull.

Unbidden, another more disturbing image flitted through his mind. That of Gus, his mentor. Gus, Skye's father. Gus, who'd gladly take up where the bull had left off, if the provocation was strong enough.

"This isn't going to work," Tyler growled. "I never should have come here."

Skye straightened, staring at him incredulously. "Look, I made a mistake. I got a little off balance. I fell. It isn't my fault that you weigh a ton."

Tyler was too weak to argue. Now that the view had shifted to a safer location, he felt his tension ease. "Sorry, I didn't mean to snap at you."

"Apology accepted." Frowning, she studied him, her expression wary. "You don't look too comfortable. Is there anything I can get you?"

All he wanted was a little space and a little peace and quiet so he could pass out in privacy. "I could use a drink. Something cold."

She nodded. "I'll be right back."

He watched her bouncy step as she strode from the room, the quick swing of her hips as she rounded the corner, and the shapely curves of her legs as she disappeared into the kitchen. He sighed, thankful for once for his incapacitated state. His willpower wasn't all that great. Weak enough, he realized, that it wouldn't matter to him whose daughter Skye might be. She'd entice any man to risk life and limb...if only he were more up to the challenge.

Slowly, his lids feeling like lead weights, he allowed his eyes to drift shut.

Sighing, Skye filled a glass to the rim with ice and water. Wearily, she brushed a hand through her hair and returned to the living room where she found Tyler sound asleep.

An unexplainable annoyance rose deep inside her as she looked down at his boyishly handsome face. Perspiration dampened his forehead, a testament to the toll his walk from the car had taken. His lips were lax, his mouth slightly open. His chest rose and fell unevenly with each breath he drew. He hadn't moved from the position in which he'd fallen, flat on his back with one blue-jean-clad knee bent skyward, the other hanging over the edge of the couch.

He looked exhausted and helpless.

It took all of her willpower not to dump the icy water onto his sleeping head.

She was apalled by her reaction. The man was injured and in pain, she told herself. But that didn't change the fact that since the moment she'd arrived at the hospital to pick him up, he'd been going out of his way to irritate her. It wasn't any wonder she felt a little out of sorts.

Resisting the urge to douse Tyler in a cold bath, Skye cooled her own temper by downing the drink in one thirsty swallow. Wiping the moisture from her lips with the back of her hand, she glanced at the sleeping man and wondered just what she was supposed to do with him.

The house was a story and a half with a large bedroom downstairs and two smaller bedrooms upstairs. Considering Tyler's incapacitated state, she thought it best if he didn't try tackling a staircase anytime soon. Which meant he had first dibs on the downstairs bed.

Skye lifted her hair against the cool breeze coming from the window's air-conditioning unit and sighed. It would be too hot to sleep upstairs. Perhaps, once she'd moved Tyler into the big bedroom, she'd camp out on the couch for the duration of his visit.

For however long that might be.

Not for the first time, she swore softly to herself, cursing her father and his inability to take on the responsibility of his friend. She shook her head, placing the empty glass on the coffee table. Thanks to Gus, she was stuck with a man who really didn't want to be with her.

A man she didn't trust herself to be alone with.

Tyler woke to the smell of dinner cooking in the oven.

Squinting at the unfamiliar ceiling, he slowly tested his limbs for mobility. While still bruised and sore, he felt somewhat less exhausted. He considered that a good sign. The light outside was fading, telling him he'd slept longer than he'd intended. He glanced at his wristwatch and was surprised to find it past six o'clock.

He'd slept away a better part of the day.

Somewhere in the house, he heard a feminine voice humming softly a country tune. Skye. Tyler smiled, feeling oddly pleased by the sound. What was the saying? *You can take the girl out of the country, but you can't take the country out of the girl.* It was reassuring to know that, for all her uppity northern ways, Skye still had her heart in Texas.

His smile faded. An unease settled over him. Staying in her house, letting her fix his meals, it all felt a little too homey. This was a temporary situation, he told himself. He'd best not get used to having a woman in his life, especially not a woman like Skye.

Gritting his teeth against the pain, he rolled over onto his side and pushed himself into a sitting position. He gave himself a moment for the room to stop spinning before he tried to stand. His back muscles cramped up on him, but he made it to his feet. Wishing he had something to lean on, Tyler shuffled into the kitchen.

The kitchen was large and spacious. In the center of the room stood an oak table and matching chairs, big enough to seat a small herd of hired hands or a growing family. The room was spotlessly clean, with a blue ceramic countertop and red tiled floors. A covered dish was warming in the oven. Beef stew, if his sense of smell was still working.

Resting a hand against the doorjamb, he pushed himself away from the kitchen entrance and went in search of Skye. Swearing softly, he felt his meager store of energy being sapped with each step he took. He found her in the dining room, sitting cross-legged amid a mess of books spread across the floor, a pen stuck behind one ear, a notebook in her hand.

She smiled when she spotted him in the doorway.

And Tyler's heart did a funny little dance in his chest.

"You're awake," she said needlessly. "And moving."

"Just barely." He leaned his weight against the arched doorjamb, trying to look nonchalant, knowing it wouldn't take much for him to fall over. Nodding his head toward the kitchen, he added, "You didn't have to make dinner."

She shrugged. "I had to eat anyway."

He didn't answer, knowing he should probably thank her. But he felt clumsy, inept, unable to find the right words.

"Dinner's almost ready," she said, unfolding the legs she had curled beneath her. "Are you hungry?"

Tyler watched as she rose to her feet. She stood barefoot and beautiful before him, asking if he were hungry. It was a loaded question, one he was certain she didn't want to hear answered. Swallowing hard, he pushed the ill-timed thoughts from his mind.

"Maybe in a little bit," he said. "I'd like to get cleaned up first."

"Do you need some help?"

Tyler nearly moaned aloud at the thought of Skye giving him a sponge bath. "No, that's okay. I'll manage."

He swayed when he pushed himself from the door frame. The room tilted drunkenly beneath his feet. Grabbing the wall for support, he closed his eyes for a minute, struggling to stop the dizziness.

"Don't be silly, Tyler. Let me help you."

His eyes flew open, as he felt the warm palm of her hand touch his arm. It felt too good to be close to her. It would be too easy to let her into his life. He clenched his teeth and said with more force than he'd intended, "I don't need your help."

She stepped back, dropping her hand, looking dazed by the impact of his harsh words.

He sighed. "Look, Skye. There's some things a man has to do on his own. As much as I'd appreciate your help, I still need my privacy."

She took another step back, distancing herself from him. "Of course. I understand."

Unfortunately, he believed she did. Just like everyone else who tried to get close, she would soon realize, that the task was impossible. He forced a grin. "So, what did ya make for dinner anyway?"

"Beef stew."

"I sure hope you didn't use your daddy's recipe. Taking varnish off the woodwork is what it's good for."

A smile flickered, then died on her lips. "Don't worry, it'll be edible."

"Yeah, well…" He glanced away, not sure which way to go.

"The bathroom's down the hall on the left. I hope you don't mind, but I took the liberty of unpacking your things while you were asleep. I stowed your shaving gear on the shelf above the sink. There should be plenty of soap and towels. Holler if you need anything."

He nodded an assent, and the motion set pinpoints of light dancing in front of his eyes.

Skye watched with a worried frown as he dragged himself from the room.

When he reached the bathroom, Tyler closed the door and nearly gave a shriek of fright when he looked into the mirror. His hair was standing on end. A knot the size of a goose egg stood out on his forehead. His jaw, gristled with a two-day beard, was swollen. Bruises, in angry shades of pink and purple, mottled his pale skin.

Good Lord, he looked worse than a drunk after an all-night bender.

Stripping off his shirt, he went about repairing the damage. In deference to his bandages, and doubting that he could stand long enough to endure a shower, he sponged down his aching body with a washcloth and hot, soapy water. Even his hair hurt when he tried to comb it. The beard was his last chore to tackle.

His legs were beginning to wobble. His hands were sweating. Even after his long nap, he felt as weak as a newborn kitten.

Breathing deeply, he dipped his head and splashed cool water on his face.

Then wished he hadn't.

The room began to spin. His head felt as though it were about to split in two with a sudden, piercing pain. His limbs began to shake uncontrollably. He reached for a handhold, anything to support him. But he only succeeded in knocking down a shelf full of toiletries. The crash reverberated throughout the room, echoing in his throbbing head.

He stumbled for the door, but couldn't quite reach the knob before his legs gave out beneath him. Slowly, he slumped to the floor, collapsing in a heap at the foot of the door. In an instant, the room faded from light to black.

Chapter Four

Skye heard the crash of glass breaking and the thump of a body hitting the floor as she stood in the kitchen, removing their dinner from the oven. Startled, she nearly dropped the covered dish on the tiled floor. For a moment, she couldn't move, rooted to the spot by fear.

Tyler had looked like death warmed over, standing in the doorway of the dining room. If he was hurt, it was her fault. She never should have let him leave without her help. Telling herself to move, she shoved the stew back into the oven and slammed the door. Tossing the oven mitts onto the counter, she ran for the bathroom.

Ever polite, she knocked before entering.

There was no response, not even a peep.

Her heart thumping loudly in her chest, she turned the knob and pushed open the door. The door moved an inch or so, then stopped, refusing to budge any further.

"Tyler," she called out, noting the strained pitch of her voice. "Can you hear me?"

A moan sounded on the other side, nearby in fact.

Frowning, she dropped to the ground and peered beneath the door. Something obstructed her view. It didn't take a genius to figure out that Tyler was blocking her entrance to the bathroom.

"Tyler, you idiot," she muttered to herself, whacking a fist on the hardwood floor, nearly hurting her hand in the process.

She scrambled to her feet and, unable to think of anything else to do, gave the door a cautious push. Tyler moaned again. And the door moved a few inches. Not much, but far enough for her to wiggle her way through the opening.

Once inside, she knelt down beside him and surveyed the damage with a frantic eye.

Shirtless, with his jeans and cowboy boots still on, Tyler looked paler than he had before, if that was at all possible. There didn't seem to be any blood spilled. Or any noticeable broken bones. His encounter with the door had roused him some. He blinked open his eyes and squinted at her.

"Skye?"

"That's right." Skye breathed a quiet sigh of relief. At least he was alive, and somewhat lucid. "How are you feeling, Tyler?"

"Like I've been hit by a truck."

"Think you can move?"

"No problem." He pushed himself to a sitting position, then petered out, thunking his head against the wall as he collapsed in defeat. "I think I'm going to need some help."

"That's what I'm here for," Skye said, feeling an odd sense of pleasure at his admission that he needed her. "Grab my arm, Tyler. I'll try to lift you, but I can't do it by myself."

She braced herself, knees bent, and struggled to lift his weight. With a little luck and a lot of work, she got him to his feet. "Good, now let's try walking."

Leaning heavily on her for support, Tyler crossed the hall, making the slow journey into the bedroom she'd already prepared for him. His bare skin felt warm, smooth and taut beneath her hands. A matting of blond hair formed a V across his chest, angling downward to disappear beneath the bandage that swathed his ribs. The clean scent of soap enveloped her as she held him close. Skye inhaled deeply, steadying herself.

Even in his injured and weakened state, Tyler was a man to be reckoned with.

They stepped into the bedroom and paused at the doorway, taking a moment to glance around the room. With a sinking heart, Skye realized there would be no easy way to get him into bed.

Repeating the drop and roll action they'd used earlier this afternoon, Tyler plopped like a deadweight in the center of the bed. This time, though, Skye caught herself before she tumbled down after him. Standing at his side, breathing heavily, she stared at him in disgust.

"The next time I ask if you need some help, don't be so stubborn and turn me down," she hollered.

"I'm sorry," he snapped. "I didn't plan on passing out."

"Yeah, well, now you know." She grabbed a booted foot and began to tug. "Let's just try and make the best of the situation. For the rest of the night, you're in bed."

The boot gave way, sending her flying backward. She regained her balance and went to work on the other foot. "Not another move unless I'm with you, got it?"

"Yes, ma'am," he muttered, closing his eyes, looking utterly defeated.

The other boot slipped off without as much resistance. She tossed the pair into the closet and picked up the Indian blanket resting at the foot of the bed. "I don't mean to be so bossy, but you scared me half to death, Tyler."

She draped the blanket across his shoulders.

He barely acknowledged the effort.

"You could have killed yourself in that bathroom," she told him.

Still, he didn't say a word.

She looked at him. "Tyler?"

His lips parted, emitting a soft snore.

Skye shook her head. It would appear Tyler had snuggled down for his second nap of the day. She watched him for a long while, assuring herself of his well-being, reluctant to leave his side.

Finally, calling herself a fool for caring, she forced herself to turn off the light and leave the room.

Tyler awoke to the clatter of dishes. Reluctantly, he pried open his eyes and found Skye standing at the foot of his bed. Hell, he moaned to himself, he wasn't dreaming, after all. He really was sharing a house with Skye.

"Rise and shine, Tyler," she said, her tone annoyingly perky, as she set a tray down at the end of the bed. "Time to eat."

The savory aroma of beef stew drifted across the room to tease his nostrils. His empty belly growled in response, reminding him that he'd slept through lunch. He placed a quieting hand on the hollow planes of his stomach. The room was almost dark, the corners thick with shadows. From the looks of it, he'd nearly slept through dinner, too.

Skye snapped on the bedside lamp, nearly blinding him.

"What time is it?" he asked, his voice gravelly with

sleep. He hooded a hand over his eyes, blocking out the worst of the glare.

"Eight o'clock," she said. Tyler caught the hint of amusement in her voice. Skye seemed to be enjoying his helplessness. "I knew you had to be hungry. I figured if I didn't wake you now, you'd be waking *me* at midnight, scrounging around my kitchen for food."

He rubbed the sleep from his eyes with a thumb and forefinger, then stole a closer look at his new roommate. She'd changed from shorts to a fire-engine-red sundress. Her dark hair was wet and slicked back from her face, as though she'd just stepped out of a shower. She smelled good, too, all powdery and sweet. Without a hint of makeup, she looked young and fresh-scrubbed.

But fine enough to tempt.

Fine enough to make a man forget he was hungry and hurtin'.

Bracing himself against the pain, Tyler dug his elbows into the soft mattress and dragged himself to a sitting position. The move took more effort than he'd imagined. Resting his head and shoulders against the heart pine headboard, he wheezed a labored breath.

Hell, the mind might be willing, but the body just wasn't cooperating.

No matter how great the incentive, this ol' cowboy wouldn't be giving in to temptation anytime soon.

Tyler shifted his weight, trying to find a comfortable spot. The movements caused the blanket to slip to his waist. The air felt unexpectedly cool against his bare skin. He touched a hand to his chest and wondered exactly what had happened to his shirt. Memories of his tumble in the bathroom, of Skye helping him into bed and tugging off his boots, flooded his mind. He snuck a cautious peek under the covers and breathed a sigh of relief to find his jeans were still in place.

Carefully, he tested his injuries. He flexed his wrist, the one Tornado had used to drag him across the arena. Still a little tender, he decided, but the swelling was down. A good sign. The cracked ribs still ached when he inhaled, but not the sharp, knife-in-your-gut kind of pain he'd experienced earlier. And his headache was down from a roar to a dull throb. The worst appeared to be over, if he didn't count his back. Pain still spasmed up and down his spine every time he moved. Tyler sighed. He supposed it would take a while before he worked out all the kinks.

"Glad to see you moving," Skye said, interrupting his thoughts.

He glanced up to find her watching him. Heat flushed his skin. Being caught unaware brought out the worst in him, making him out of sorts, ornery.

"Why, Skye," he drawled, flexing a brow Groucho Marx style, hiding his embarrassment behind an attempt at humor. "I didn't know you cared."

"Care might be too strong a word," she said. Picking up a pillow, she fluffed it a little too vigorously, her nervous actions belying her confident tone. "Let's just say you'd have put a heck of a crimp in my plans for the summer, if you'd decided not to remain in the land of the living. Funeral arrangements would have set me back a good two...maybe three days in my work schedule."

"Don't hold back now, Skye," he growled, unable to ignore the burr of annoyance the carefree words brought him. "If my being here's an inconvenience, just say so."

"I never said you were an inconvenience, Tyler." She sighed. "All I meant was...the faster you recuperate, the faster—"

"You'll be rid of me," he finished for her, scowling.

One hand holding the pillow, one hand on her hip, she glared at him. "I was going to say...the faster you'll be back on the rodeo circuit."

The reminder of the tenuous state of his career in the rodeo sealed his cantankerous mood for the night.

Oblivious to his tetchy state of mind, she drew closer. And Tyler's muscles tightened reflexively. With a cool hand on his shoulder, she gently urged him to lean forward, far enough so she could plop the pillow behind his back. Pain ricocheted up and down his spine at the simple movement. A pain sharp enough to force him to swear in sheer agony.

"Dammit, Skye. Be careful. What are you trying to do? Kill me?"

"I-I'm sorry," she said, dropping her hand, taking a step back as though she'd been struck.

Instantly guilt washed over him. He closed his eyes and muttered another oath under his breath. Slowly, he opened his eyes and faced his punishment. "No, I'm the one who should be sorry. I should be thanking you, not growling at you like a grizzly bear."

"That's okay," she said, making him feel even more guilty with her understanding. "It's hard to feel cordial when you're in pain."

Tyler bit back the urge to argue the point. He had a lot of male pride sloshing around inside him, he reminded himself. It was only natural that being beholden to a woman—especially a woman as beautiful as Skye—for his every need grated against his male ego.

But it was more than that, he admitted. The truth was, he just didn't know how to act around a woman.

Outside the bedroom, that is.

Pleasing a woman in bed came as easy to him as breathing. The problem was, when entertaining a lady, he'd never stuck around long enough to be bothered with more than a little mood-setting pillow talk and a "thank you, ma'am," once the night was over.

This cowboy made it a habit to be long gone before the dawn's early light.

Now, he was faced with an indefinite stay with a woman with whom—if the circumstances were different—he'd be more than happy to share his bed. Unfortunately, that just wasn't going to happen. If he wanted to survive the ordeal with his sanity and his pride intact, he was going to have to do some serious rethinking on his approach in handling the opposite sex.

"How about some dinner?" Skye asked, drawing him out of his disturbing thoughts.

"If it isn't too much trouble," he said, determined to reform his misguided ways, ready to show at least a modicum of gratitude toward Skye.

"No trouble at all." She set the tray across his lap. Shaking open a napkin, she settled it over his chest. Her fingertips grazed his bare skin, setting off a brushfire of tingling delight.

Tyler nearly moaned again. This time, pain had nothing to do with his reaction. His libido was suffering something awful. One way or another, he told himself, Skye Whitman was going to be the death of him.

"Are you feeling okay?" she asked, her brow wrinkling into a frown. "You're looking kind of funny."

"I'm fine," he said through gritted teeth.

"Because if you're not, I could—"

"Skye, I'm just real hungry," he said, aiming for a little space. Having her within reachin'-out-and-grabbin' distance was putting a strain on his self-control. He might be in pain, but he wasn't dead, after all.

"Of course, you are," she said, tsking. He half ex-

pected her to croon, "You poor baby." She didn't, thank
God. Instead, she sat down on the bed next to him, picked
up a utensil and tried to spoonfeed him his dinner.

Good intentions forgotten, angry pride exploded deep
inside him. "For Pete's sake, Skye. I'm not a complete
invalid. The bull didn't break my arms. The last time I
looked, I still had full use of both limbs."

A rosy hue blossomed on her cheeks. The spoon slipped
from her fingers, clanging noisily onto the tray. She rose
to her feet and glared at him. "There's no need to shout,
Tyler," she hollered. "All I was trying to do was help."

Tyler closed his eyes against the anger in her tone. So
much for being grateful, he chided himself, giving himself
a mental kick in the pants. For the life of him, he didn't
understand why he had to go out of his way to antagonize
the one person in the world who'd cared enough to show
him a little concern. He was acting like the storybook lion
with a thorn in his paw. Only, unlike the fable, he'd rather
suffer in not-too-quiet silence, than allow anyone—especially Skye—to help him.

Opening his eyes, he sighed in defeat. "Skye—"

She held up a quieting hand. "That's okay, Tyler. I
might be a little slow, but I can take a hint. I'll just leave
you to your dinner. Holler when you're finished. I'll be
down the hall...working."

With that, she turned to leave.

But not before he caught a glimpse of her big blue eyes,
all shiny and moist with emotion—anger...or wounded
pride, he wasn't sure which.

An unexpected reaction surged deep inside of Tyler.
One he didn't quite understand. Panic pure and simple.

He didn't want her to go.

"Skye, wait."

Her step faltered at his pleading tone. She blinked hard,

embarrassed by the tell-tale moisture leaking from the corners of her eyes. Not trusting herself, not trusting Tyler, she kept her back to him, one foot poised to run. "What is it, Tyler?"

"I—um—don't want you to go," he said, his voice low and gruff.

The admission shocked her. She wasn't sure what she'd expected. An apology, perhaps, but not a plea for her to stay. Briskly, she wiped the tears from her eyes and turned to face him.

He still wore a pout on his face that would have made a three year old envious. His beard-stubbled chin was set in a stubborn line. He kept his eyes on his tray of food, as though he were too embarrassed—or too obstinate—to face her. For a moment, she wondered if she'd imagined the desperation in his tone.

"What did you say?" she asked.

"You're not going to make this easy, are you?" he asked, releasing a breath through clenched teeth. He looked at her then, his soft brown eyes revealing nothing but sincerity. "I said...don't go, not yet."

Her heart gave an uneven little thump in her chest. She hesistated, not trusting herself to speak.

With a nod of his head, he motioned to the bentwood rocker near the bed. "I could use the company. Why don't you stay with me for a while...please."

Please. Skye sighed. She'd always been a sucker for a man in need. Striving for nonchalance, she lifted her shoulders in a delicate shrug and said, "I suppose I could spare a minute or two."

A chagrined look crossed his face. He opened his mouth, looking ready to bite out another sharp comeback. But he must have thought better of it. The pout still firmly in place, he picked up the forgotten spoon and dug into his stew.

Her legs still trembling, she gratefully sank down onto the cushioned seat of the rocking chair. Warily, she studied him, wondering how long this unspoken truce would last. She waited, letting him be the first to speak.

He took his time before striking up a conversation. Around his second bite of food, he asked the one question for which she didn't know if she had an answer. "You haven't been home for a long time, Skye. What made you decide to spend your summer in Texas?"

She bit her lip, considering her answer, unwilling to blurt out the truth. That after six years of being on her own, she'd become homesick. "I'm not sure. I suppose it was because this is my last chance to come back. Once the summer's over, Ralph will be back from Europe—"

"Ralph," he said with a disgusted look, as though his last bite of stew hadn't agreed with him.

She'd had enough lectures on Ralph's deficiencies from her father that she didn't need to hear them from Tyler. Ignoring his sour expression, she continued, "And, of course, once I'm finished with my thesis, I'll be looking for a job."

"I guess that means you'll be job hunting up north, so's you can be close to Ralph."

She wasn't sure if it was his sarcastic tone, or his assumption to know her plans, but Skye felt a prickling of annoyance. "Well, that would be the smart thing to do, seeing how we're planning to get married."

"Yeah, that would be the smart thing to do." He jabbed his spoon at a chunk of carrot. "I'm sure Gus must be disappointed you won't be living and working in Texas."

"He hasn't really said," she admitted, crossing her legs, her fingers fidgeting along the hem of her skirt.

The truth be told, she and Gus had always lived such separate lives, even from the time she was just a small child. While he'd kept tabs on her, inquiring after her welfare and feigning the role of a doting father, they both knew it was an obligatory show of concern. Gus was a cowboy at heart. He'd chosen the independent life of the rodeo over his daughter. She doubted if he would care what she did now.

"He does worry about you," Tyler said softly.

Startled, Skye lifted her gaze to find Tyler studying her, a thoughtful expression on his face. She squirmed uncomfortably in her seat, unnerved by how close he came to echoing her thoughts.

"Hell, for the last six years, all I've ever heard is Skye this, and Skye that…the man's a broken record when it comes to braggin' about you."

"That's funny," she said, giving a bitter-sounding chuckle. "All he ever talks about when he calls me is your latest standing on the rodeo circuit."

An uncomfortable silence fell between them.

Tyler was the first to break the tension, shifting gears quick enough to give her whiplash. "So, Skye," he drawled the words, layering them with a thick, cowboy twang, "why don't you tell me about ol' Ralph?"

"Ralph?" she squeaked, her throat feeling suddenly dry. She didn't want to discuss Ralph with anyone—most especially with Tyler. Tyler was Texan through and through. He was bigger than life and handsome to boot. Any man, even someone as gentle and supportive as Ralph, would pale in comparison to a champion rodeo star.

She narrowed a suspicious gaze. "Why do you want to know about Ralph?"

"Why?" He shrugged, looking the picture of innocence. "Because it's my job to keep an eye on you."

"Your job?"

"We've known each other for a long time. We're practically family," he reminded her, a devilish glint surfacing in the depths of his brown eyes. "You said it yourself, Skye. I'm like a brother to you."

"Brother, ha! You're more like an uninvited relative that's always hanging around," she blurted out without thinking. She clapped a hand to her mouth, appalled by what she'd just said.

Tyler's assessing gaze never left her embarrassment-warmed face. "Now that's the second time you've alluded to my unwanted presence. Keep it up, Skye, and I might get a complex."

Heat suffused her cheeks. "I'm sorry, Tyler. I didn't mean—"

"No, I think you meant it exactly the way it sounded." He pushed his half-eaten bowl of stew away, sighing deeply. "Hell, Skye, I'm not stupid. I know that all the time your daddy spent teaching me the ropes of bull riding meant he had that much less time to spend with you. It's only normal that you'd feel a little resentful."

"It wasn't your fault," she murmured.

"Neither was it yours. Gus makes his own decisions."

Another strained silence lapsed between them.

Skye nearly shouted her relief when the phone rang, interrupting the tenuous conversation. She leaned forward, reaching for the bedside phone.

Closer by an arm's width, Tyler beat her to the punch. He picked up the receiver, cradling it against his shoulder. With his deep, Texas twang, he drawled an easy, "Hello."

Skye frowned, watching him as an amused expression flitted across his face.

"No, you've got the right number. This is the Whitman ranch," he said. He glanced at Skye, his smile deepening. "Who am I? Why, I'm Tyler Bradshaw, an old friend of the family."

Skye brought a hand to her head, rubbing the dull pain that throbbed against her temples. *Please, God,* she recited in silent prayer, *don't let it be—*

"Ralph? You don't say. We were just talking about you. Skye's right here." Tyler cupped a hand across the mouthpiece, extending the phone to her. "It's long distance...the professor." He raised a brow, giving her a quizzical look. "He seems a little confused. Didn't you tell him you had a houseguest?"

Skye didn't move. She stared at the phone, too numb to react. Of course, she hadn't told Ralph about Tyler's visit. She'd hoped to keep Tyler's stay at the ranch as quiet as possible. Not that Ralph didn't trust her. It was just...she didn't see the need to upset him. She didn't know how to make him understand why she hadn't mentioned Tyler's name before if he was such an old friend of the family.

"If you don't want to talk to him, I could make an excuse," Tyler offered helpfully.

"No," she said, rising to her feet. "You've done enough already, thank you. If you don't mind, I'd like a little privacy. I'll take the call in the kitchen." She stopped midway to the door, eyeing him with a suspicious glance. "You will hang up the phone, won't you?"

"Me?" He touched a hand to his bare chest, his look one of self-righteous indignation. "Now look, Skye, I may have a few faults—"

"A few?"

Ignoring her outburst, he continued, "Eavesdropping isn't one of them."

"Right," she said, striding to the door. "Just eat your dinner. I'll be back in a few minutes to collect the tray."

Just what she needed, she muttered to herself, a cowboy suffering from a moral sense of outrage.

Tyler's twisted sense of honor was the last thing she should be worried about, she told herself, as she hurried to the kitchen, her bare feet slapping against the hardwood floor. She had more important matters to consider. Such as what she was going to tell Ralph about a certain cowboy staying at her house.

And why, if she hadn't spoken to her intended for two long days, wasn't she more thrilled at the prospect of talking to him now?

The skirt of Skye's sundress fluttered about her thighs as she disappeared around the corner of the doorway. Her bare feet fell lightly against the wooden floor, the sound fading as she moved farther away from him. Reluctantly, Tyler pressed his ear to the phone and listened to the click of the extension being picked up in the kitchen. He ignored the hollow ache in his chest as he heard Skye's soft, lilting voice greet her fiancé.

"Hi, Ralph. I'm so glad you called...."

Slowly, Tyler replaced the receiver in its cradle. He stared at the phone for a long moment, wishing he hadn't been so quick to assure Skye of his trustworthy qualities. Tyler almost smiled. Right now, he'd give his favorite pair of cowboy boots to hear what excuse Skye was cookin' up for ol' Ralph.

Obviously, Skye was keeping secrets from her intended.

He wondered why.

Scowling, he grabbed his spoon and pushed the thought from his mind. Skye's motives were none of his business. He was a temporary houseguest, nothing more. The less he got involved in her affairs the better.

Affairs. The thought caused an uneasy reaction in his throat, like a lump too big to swallow. An unwanted picture of Skye in the arms of another man flickered in his mind's eye. The spoon clattered as he dropped it back onto the tray. Not surprisingly, he'd lost his appetite.

Unsuccessfully, he tried not to listen to the murmur of her voice as it drifted down the hall. Each soft sound brought a sharp reminder that she was a woman who was already taken. She belonged to someone else. She was off limits to him.

Minutes passed like hours before Skye returned to the bedroom. When he heard the padding of her footsteps against the hallway's hardwood floor, Tyler picked up his spoon and pretended an interest in his dinner.

Skye breezed in, looking flushed and beautiful—a woman in love.

Tyler scowled. "So, how's Ralph?"

"He's fine," she said, her voice a little too light and carefree. She took her seat in the rocker, giving a nervous-sounding laugh. "Just busy, busy, busy."

"Being a history professor must be real tough."

"Yes, it is," she said, ignoring the sarcasm in his tone. "Ralph spends a lot of time reading and researching. He works hard. And he's very ambitious. Someday, he wants to head the History Department."

"I see," he said, picking up a flaky biscuit off the tray. A noncommittal observation. Not a hint of censure. Nor a hint of approval, either. Tyler prided himself on his ability to keep his emotions in line.

"He's reliable, too," Skye enthused, waxing eloquent

the virtues of Ralph Breedlow. "I can always count on him to be there when I need him."

"A regular Boy Scout," Tyler drawled, crumbling the biscuit between two fingers, feeling his self-control slip away. "I guess that's why you forgot to tell him about my staying with you at the ranch...because he's so dependable."

"Are you going to eat that food, or play with it, Tyler?" she asked, her temper flaring.

"No need to get mad, Skye." He chuckled, holding up his hands in mock surrender. "I was just curious about why you never mentioned our little arrangement to Ralph."

She raised her chin, shaking her hair out of her eyes. "I didn't think it was important."

"Not important?" His smile faded. "You have another man living in your house and answering your phone. How'd you explain that to your fiancé?"

"I told him the truth. That you were an old and dear friend of my father's. Emphasis on the old."

"So in other words...you lied."

"Not a lie, exactly. Just a slight exaggeration of the facts." She frowned, looking at the tray of food. "Tyler, you haven't eaten much."

"I'm not very hungry," he said, grimacing as he shifted his weight against the pillows.

"Are you still in pain?" she asked, her tone softening.

Tyler stubbornly refused to answer. As much as he enjoyed Skye's company, the conversation was sapping him of his meager store of strength. His ribs were beginning to ache. His hand was beginning to swell up again. And no matter how hard he tried to hide it, he couldn't move his back without pain rearing its ugly head. But he'd be damned if he'd admit as much to Skye.

"The doctor sent painkillers and some muscle relaxants for your back. I'll get them for you."

"No," he said, his tone brusque.

"It wouldn't be any trouble," she said, misunderstanding his impatience for not wanting to be a bother. She rose to her feet. "They're just in the kitchen. It'll only take a second."

He grabbed her wrist, stopping her. "I said I don't need any medicine."

Her wrist looked small encircled by his big hand. Her skin felt warm and smooth. He felt the frightened tremble of her hand beneath his touch. Reflexively, he loosened his grip on her wrist, but he didn't release her.

"Tyler, don't be silly," she chided, giving him a nervous smile. "Now isn't the time to prove how macho you are. I promise, I won't think any less of you if you need a little help to take the edge off your pain."

"You don't understand, Skye," he said, releasing an impatient breath. Slowly, he released his grip, letting her slip away.

"You're right, I don't." Her smile faded. She sat down again on the chair, studying him. "Maybe you ought to explain."

Tyler sighed, lifting a hand to rub the grit of tiredness from his eyes. Instinct told him to close ranks, put up his guard. Not many people knew his life story...for a good reason. He didn't like the idea of getting too close, of sharing confidences with others.

Risking his privacy meant risking his heart.

Despite the warning signals tripping through his mind, he found himself unable to stop the words of explanation from flowing. "My pa was an alcoholic," he said, noting the strained, uneven sound of his voice. He cleared his throat. "He spent more time in the taverns, than he did at home or at a job."

"I'm sorry, Tyler. I didn't know. That must have been hard on you and your mother—"

"My mother couldn't take it. She left home when I was eleven years old. I stuck it out until I was seventeen...until I couldn't stand watching the old man drink himself to death."

Skye didn't say a word. Her expression remained coolly neutral as she patiently waited for him to continue.

Tyler gave a mirthless laugh. "The funny thing is, once I was on my own, I spent a lot of time in bars getting drunk myself. It didn't take me long to see the writing on the wall. By the time I was twenty, I knew I was well on my way to repeating my father's mistakes."

Skye shook her head. "Tyler, you don't have to—"

He held up a quieting hand. "I swear to you, Skye, I haven't touched a drop of liquor or a single pill—prescribed or otherwise—since. And I don't intend to start up again now. So if you don't mind, I'd just as soon you throw those painkillers in the trash, where they belong."

She studied him for a long moment without saying a word. Then softly, she said, "All right."

He looked at her, lifting a brow in question, surprised that she hadn't put up even a token argument. His chest tightened when he saw a dangerous glint of admiration reflected in her eyes.

Careful not to jar the bed, she picked up the food tray. "I'll just leave you to get some rest now. If there's anything else I can do—"

He shook his head. "No, I'll be fine."

"Tyler," she said, releasing an impatient breath. "You're not fine. You've been dragged by a bull. So don't be so stubborn. If you need anything—anything at all—just tell me. I'll be down the hall the whole night.''

Tyler didn't answer. The thought of her being so close unnerved him.

She left him then. With a quick smile and a soft goodnight, she strode to the door. Tyler held himself still, listening to her soft footsteps in the hallway. The sound faded, and all that was left was the lingering aroma of Skye's powdery scent.

He inhaled deeply, wondering why the room suddenly felt so empty.

Chapter Five

"Skye?"

Tyler's voice echoed down the hall, making its way into the dining room where Skye sat at her computer, staring at a blank screen.

"Skye?" he called again, a touch of impatience this time.

Skye closed her eyes and counted to ten, struggling to hold on to the last vestiges of her much-needed patience. Three days had passed since Tyler had arrived on her doorstep. Three days in which she'd gone beyond the call of nursing duties. From a glass of water for a parched throat, to a heating pad for his back, or just a little assistance rearranging his pillows, he'd taken to heart her encouragement to "holler" if he needed help.

Tyler had gone from pushing her away to becoming a demanding patient.

Needless to say, she was getting diddly-squat done on her thesis.

"Why me?" she muttered. The legs of the chair rasped

against the wooden floor as she surged to her feet. "Why couldn't Tyler have picked a different state to get himself thrown off of a bull. Say, Oklahoma...or Arizona? Why'd he have to pick my backyard to do the honors?"

"Skye, is that you?" Tyler hollered. "What did ya say? I can't hear ya."

"I said, I'll be right there," Skye called out through clenched teeth.

She drew in a deep breath, willing herself to be calm as she slowly made her way to Tyler's bedroom. It wasn't his fault that he was helpless, she told herself. He was a man, after all. Pain and illness brought out the child in all men.

Though she had a sneaking suspicion it was more than pain that ailed Tyler. Her step faltered. The truth was, she suspected he might be mildly depressed. These last few days, he'd become apathetic, showing little interest in anything other than driving her to distraction. He didn't even care about his recovery. No amount of coaxing on her part could get him up and out of his bed, let alone risk a smile.

Not that she blamed him.

She hesitated at the door of his bedroom, leaning a shoulder against the doorframe. Listening to the drone of the television, she gave herself a moment for the knots in her stomach to untangle before she faced him again. Up until a few days ago, Tyler was an active, physical man who was used to pushing his body to the limits of endurance. Now he was weak and dependent. It wasn't any wonder that he'd have a tough time accepting the fact that he wasn't invincible.

The problem was—as far as she could see—Tyler would just as soon spit in the wind than admit he was feeling a little down. Any consolation she'd be able to give him would have to be done on the sly. He wouldn't accept it any other way.

Fortified with new purpose—getting Tyler back on the road to recovery and out of the too-close confines of her house—Skye pushed herself from the door frame and strode into his bedroom. Two steps into the room, she stopped dead in her tracks.

In deference to the heat, Tyler had tossed the bedcovers aside. He'd also traded his disreputable pair of blue jeans for a cool pair of shorts that showed off his long, muscular legs to an unfair advantage. Shirtless and now pantless, he struck a formidable pose. Formidable enough to take her breath away.

Good heavens, but he was a fine specimen of mankind.

Skye drew in a ragged breath and regrouped her waning strength. What was wrong with her? She was an engaged woman. She shouldn't be having prurient thoughts about another man. Especially not Tyler Bradshaw, the heart-breaker of the rodeo circuit.

The reminder cooled her raging hormones. The man already had scores of women across the country lusting after his body, as it was. She'd never be able to live down the humiliation if he knew she was among their ranks.

"What took you so long?" he grumbled.

"I was busy, Tyler…working on my thesis. You remember my thesis. That little paper I'm supposed to be finishing this summer. Of course, at the rate I'm going, it'll be December before I'm done."

He looked at her, his eyes narrow slits of ill-temperedness.

She heaved a frustrated sigh. "What is it this time, Tyler?"

"Something's wrong with this dang thing," he said, holding up the TV's remote control. "I think it's busted."

In a fit of kindness—not to mention, desperation—she'd pushed the house's one and only aging television into Tyler's bedroom in the hopes of giving the poor man something to do. She'd regretted the decision ever since. Day and night, the noise of the TV blared down the hall. Soaps, talk shows, sporting events—Tyler watched them all with an indiscriminate eye. At the speed he was channel surfing, she doubted if he was really paying attention to the shows. The television served more as companion noise than real entertainment.

"I just put in a new set of batteries," she said, frowning.

"Well, they're not working now," he said in an annoyingly matter-of-fact voice.

Skye snatched the remote from his hand, careful to avoid any physical contact. Her willpower was at an all-time low. She didn't need to test its weakened endurance. Pointing the remote at the TV, she punched in buttons and...nothing happened. She smacked it against her palm, wishing it was Tyler's head she were whacking some sense into, but the remote remained stubbornly uncooperative.

She tossed the broken gadget onto the bed. "You're right, Tyler. It's busted."

"Now how am I supposed to change the channel?" he growled.

"Here's a thought. You could get out of bed," she said, trying not to sound as irritable as she felt.

"I don't know about that, Skye." He flexed his shoulders, cringing noticeably at the effort. "My back's still feelin' kind of punk. I don't think I should be straining it any more than I have to."

"Then what would you suggest, Tyler? That I stay in

here with you and change the channel whenever you want?''

He rubbed his chin, scratching the stubbly growth of his beard, actually considering the possibility.

She stamped a foot on the hardwood floor, tapping out an angry warning beat.

''Nah, that's okay,'' he said, taking the hint. ''I guess I don't feel much like watching television, after all.''

''Good.'' She marched over to the TV and snapped off the set. Silence descended upon the room. Skye breathed a sigh of relief. Finally, she would get a little peace and quiet. The tension melted from her muscles.

Until she faced Tyler again.

Reclining lazily against the bed pillows, looking disheveled and sexy, he studied her with an expectant glint in his eye. Her stomach did a funny little flip-flop. Good Lord, what was she going to do to entertain him now?

''Would you like a book to read?'' she asked.

''A book?'' he drawled, looking doubtful.

''You know, that thing with words typed on its pages,'' she said slowly, enunciating each word with care.

''I know what a book is, Skye.'' His jaw tightened. A vein pulsed at his temple. Obviously, Tyler was not amused. ''I may not have a couple of college degrees to my name, but that doesn't mean I can't read.''

''Of course it doesn't,'' she said, feeling a wash of embarrassment stain her face. She'd spoken without thinking, allowing her impatience and frustration to affect her judgment. She'd wanted to help Tyler, not make him feel worse. ''I didn't mean to imply—''

''I'm sure you didn't,'' he said, cutting her off, averting his gaze. ''Look, Skye. I'm kind of tired. If it's all the same to you, I think I'll take a nap.''

"Um, sure," she said, backstepping toward the door. "I'll just leave you...."

The words died on her lips. She'd almost made her escape, had almost found sanctuary from his unnerving presence, when she gave him one last look. He was staring unblinkingly at the blank TV screen, feigning a bored expression. But his eyes told a different story. In their depths there was a flicker of unexpected emotion...sadness mixed with uncertainty.

Belatedly, she remembered her resolve to cheer Tyler up, to give him a gentle push out of that blue funk that seemed to have enveloped him.

So much for helping out a friend in need.

"Tyler," she said, lingering at the doorway.

He glanced at her, his expression prohibitive.

She swallowed hard and continued. "I think you need a change of scenery."

Tyler gave a short, humorless laugh. "What did you have in mind, Skye? A trip to the Bahamas?"

"No," she said, gritting her teeth in exasperation. No matter how ungrateful he might be, she must remember Tyler was a man in pain. "I was thinking more in terms of dinner on the patio."

"Hell, Skye, it's got to be ninety-five in the shade. And you want to eat outside?" He gave a dismissive shake of his head. "It's too damned hot."

"Not at seven o'clock in the evening. The sun will be starting to set by then. It'll be cooler outside."

He set his jaw in an uncompromising line. "Yeah, well, I'm not exactly mobile."

"I'm not asking you to run laps in the backyard, Tyler," she insisted, unable to keep the edge from her tone. "All you have to do is sit in a chair and eat."

He looked at her, remaining stubbornly mute.

Bullying him wasn't working, but she knew Tyler had a weakness for women. Perhaps it was time she used her feminine wiles.

Layering on the sugar and spice, she said, "Tyler, I wish you'd change your mind. You'd be doing me a favor. It's—" Her voice faltered. She bit her lip, uncertain whether or not she could carry off this farce. Batting her eyes to hide her own doubts, she gave him what she hoped was an encouraging smile. "It's been awfully lonely out here on the ranch. I was hoping you'd keep me company while I ate my dinner."

Tyler leaned back against the bed pillows and muttered a few choice expletives under his breath.

Skye waited, not daring to speak.

He glared at her. "If I say yes, will you leave me alone so I can get some shut-eye?"

"Why, of course, Tyler," she said, her smile deepening. "Whatever you want. Just say the word."

His expression shifted, from moody to considering. Head to toe, he caressed her with an assessing gaze, lingering long enough on the curves of her breasts and hips to make her squirm uncomfortably. "Careful, Skye," he said finally. "You'd best not be making promises you don't intend to keep. What I really want might surprise you."

His meaning was clear.

What he wanted was her.

If he were in better shape, she'd be more worried. As it was, his innuendo sent a hot flush of discomfort through her body. Not because she was appalled by the idea.

But rather, because she was intrigued.

Without another word, she turned and fled the room, wondering, not for the first time since Tyler had moved in, if she'd taken on more than she could handle.

* * *

Tyler wasn't sure if he could handle being an invalid for much longer.

That was what he told himself, breathing in the sweet scent of Skye's perfume as she helped settle him into one of the wrought-iron chairs on the patio at the rear of the house. Grudgingly, Tyler acknowledged that he wasn't bouncing back from his injuries as he'd expected. Hell, the last time he'd hurt his back, it had taken him only a day or two to iron out the kinks. It had been over four days since the bull had thrown him, and he still felt as bent and bruised as though it had happened yesterday.

His gaze lingered on Skye's ample curves. He sighed. It seemed such an awful waste to have a woman as desirable as Skye less than an arm's length away, and not be able to do a dang thing about it.

"How are you feeling?" Skye asked, making him wonder if she could read his mind. "Comfy?"

Skye had lined the chair with pillows and cushions, layering on the softness until he felt as though he were sitting on a big marshmallow.

"Just great," he said, keeping his tone flat, revealing none of the frustration which bubbled just beneath the surface.

She smiled, looking pleased. "Then I'll get us some drinks. Tea, okay?"

"Tea's fine," he said, frowning.

Her smile faltered. A pensive line formed on her brow.

Tyler watched her warily, waiting for her to leave. He didn't care how hungry he was, if she fussed over him one more time, he was going to hobble right back to his bedroom, dinner or no dinner.

"Tea, it is," she said with a quick nod of approval. "I'll be back in a flash."

Her sandals scraped against the concrete floor, drawing his attention to the slender curves of her legs. The cotton material of her shorts hugged her thighs as she strode determinedly toward the house. Late evening sunlight streaming through the branches of the shade tree dappled the bare skin of her arms. She looked pretty and inviting, a tempting treat on a hot summer's eve.

Tyler slammed the brakes on the direction his thoughts were taking. Skye was becoming more of a problem than he'd ever thought possible. She was fast becoming another hitch on his road to recovery.

In the hospital, when he'd been woozy from his head injury, he'd mistakenly believed he could handle living in close proximity to Skye. So what if she was a deadly combination of unassuming beauty and spunky energy? She was Gus's daughter, the closest thing he'd ever had to a real family. Certainly he had enough willpower to resist the temptation of a woman who considered him a brother.

He was wrong, of course.

Every minute he spent with her was just another reminder of how dim-witted he really was. Even in his weakened state, it took every bit of his strength to keep his hands to himself whenever she was near. More than once, he'd been sorely tempted to reach out and see for himself if her skin was as soft as it appeared, or if her dark, shiny hair would be silky to the touch, or if her strawberry-colored lips tasted as good as he'd remembered.

The whinny of a horse broke into his thoughts, saving him from torturing himself any further. From his spot at the patio table, he had a perfect view of the barn and paddocks. The ranch wasn't a working ranch, per se. Gus kept a few horses stabled in the barn to ride whenever the mood struck. Jack Austin, a former rodeo buddy, took care of the small band of quarter horses in exchange for room and board.

The rest of the ranch had fallen upon hard times from sheer neglect. From where he sat, Tyler could see fences that needed mending, pastures that were going to seed, and a barn and house that were both in need of a couple coats of paint. He shook his head. He didn't understand why Gus kept the place. It was a shame to let it become such an eyesore.

The ranch was in dire need of a firm and caring hand to whip it back into shape. With a little determination and a lot of hard work, it could be a showcase. The perfect place for a cowboy to settle down, find himself a pretty little wife—

"Do you like your tea sweet?" Skye asked, startling him.

"No," he said, shaking all thoughts of domesticity from his mind. "I like things simple, uncomplicated."

"It's only tea." With a laugh, she set the frosty glass on the table before him, then took a seat across from him. "How complicated can it be?"

"You'd be surprised," he said, taking a thirsty swig of the cold drink.

Settling down…pretty little wife—where the hell did those ideas come from? Staying here with Skye was doing some mighty strange things to his head. Why else would he be considering the pros and cons of matrimonial bliss? He was dangerously close to overstaying his visit. It didn't matter how weak he felt, the sooner he was movin' on the better, he told himself, wiping his clammy palms on his jeans-clad legs.

He glanced down at his jeans—his foolish attempt to impress—and almost laughed aloud. In honor of the occasion, he'd decided to dress for dinner. Somewhere in his duffel bag, he'd found a clean pair of jeans and a T-shirt that didn't have any rips or holes—not an easy feat for a cowboy who spent most of his days on the road and wasn't privy to the conveniences of a washer and dryer at home.

Not that Skye would know the difference. He doubted if she understood or, for that matter, cared what life on the rodeo circuit was really like.

"When's the last time you went riding?" he asked, nodding toward the horse barn, steering the conversation in a safer direction.

She laughed, a light, airy sound that tickled his ears. "It's been quite a few years since I've been on the back of a horse."

"It's like riding a bike," he assured her. "Once you learn, you never forget."

"Is that right?" she asked, angling a wry glance his way. "Here I thought being a greenhorn meant I'd have a better chance of being tossed off on my—" She smiled, her eyes sparkling with mischief. "Well, you know."

Unable to stop himself, he returned her smile. He couldn't help it. No matter how hard he tried to fight it, Skye had a way of making him feel at ease. Talking to her, listening to her sass her way through a conversation, it felt as though he'd come home after a long absence.

Lord, he hadn't realized how much he'd missed having her around.

"To tell you the truth, I have been thinking about riding again," Skye admitted, breaking into his thoughts. "Jack—you know, Gus's friend who's been taking care of the horses—he's been telling me he could use some help exercising them. He says Gus doesn't come out often enough to do them justice."

"Then you should do it," Tyler urged. "It'd be good for you to get outside in the fresh air. You've been cooped up inside all week."

"Yeah, well." She shrugged. "I've been busy...."

The words faded, the thought left incomplete.

"You've been busy because I've made you so," he finished for her after a moment's hesitation. Raking a hand through his blond hair, he growled with frustration. "Hell, Skye. I don't know why you put up with me. I've been acting worse than an ol' grizzly bear needin' a winter's nap."

"You've been hurt, Tyler." She ran a delicate finger over the rim of her glass, collecting beads of moisture. When she licked away the drops with the tip of her tongue, Tyler felt his body tighten in response. Oblivious to his, literally, growing awareness, she gave a wistful sigh. "You aren't yourself. I realize that."

He didn't say a word, not trusting himself to answer. It didn't take much for Skye to turn him into a blubbering idiot.

She looked at him, frowning slightly. "Are you all right, Tyler? Sitting outside isn't too much for you, is it?"

"N-no." His voice broke. He hid his discomfort behind a quick clearing of his throat. "I'm fine. Just hungry, that's all."

"That I can fix." A pair of dimples danced in her cheeks as she blessed him with a smile. She stood with catlike grace, placing her drink on the table. "I'll be right back with our dinner. Don't go away."

He forced a smile, chuckling politely at her attempt at humor. As soon as she disappeared through the kitchen door, however, his smile faded into a grimace.

He was being punished.

For all the women he'd blissfully enjoyed throughout

the years. For all the times he'd accepted the pleasure their warm bodies and soothing ways brought. For all the shattered hopes and wounded hearts he'd left behind, he was now being punished for his past sins.

What else could explain this little part of hell that he was being forced to endure?

Skye was the epitome of womanly perfection. The thought of indulging himself with her compact curves, soft skin and sweet lips made his body thrum with a lusty anticipation. She was more of a temptation than this cowboy could handle.

But handle it he must.

For the first time in his life, there was more at stake than instant physical gratification. Make a move on Skye, and he'd be risking more than a well-deserved dressing-down by Gus, Skye's daddy.

He'd be risking the heart of a woman who considered him a friend.

"What do you mean cowboys are running away from their feminine side?" Tyler demanded. His brows dipped into a deep frown. "What feminine side?"

Skye nearly laughed aloud at the indignant expression on his face. "I'm talking about the nurturing side, Tyler, the need to settle down, procreate and thrive. Everyone's born with the instinct to nest...even men. Though you wouldn't be able to tell by the 'boys' traveling on the rodeo circuit."

He narrowed a suspicious glance. "Is this one of those philosophy theories of yours?"

"No, Tyler, it's just a personal observation of mine."

"What makes you think we're running away from anything?" He scowled. "It takes a lot of guts for a man to sit on top of two thousand pounds of man-eating bull."

"Guts…or stupidity," she said, sitting back in her chair, waiting for his reaction, knowing she'd finally struck a nerve.

Since the beginning of their dinner, she'd been hacking away, trying to break through that glum mood of his. It had been days since she'd seen him quite so animated as he was at that moment. While the bruises on his face were still prominent, a healthy flush of color had returned to his cheeks. His eyes flashed with emotion. Energy seemed to pulsate through his veins. One way or another, she'd found a way to prod Tyler out of the blues.

She just hoped she would survive the fallout of his self-righteous outrage.

Tyler pushed away the remains of his dinner—chicken and dumplings—and leaned forward, elbows on the table-top. "I guess you'd prefer somebody smart and cultured… like your Ralph."

Skye frowned, shifting uncomfortably in her seat. Somehow, the conversation had changed direction, becoming much too personal for her taste. "I'd rather not talk about Ralph."

"Something wrong with your fiancé?"

"No, there's nothing wrong with my fiancé," she snapped. "It's just…"

She stopped, unwilling to allow her temper to ruin a perfect evening.

"Just…" he prompted, refusing to let go.

She sighed. "It's just…whenever you or Gus talk about him, you have a way of making Ralph sound foolish."

"Why, Skye, I assure you, if I've made Ralph appear foolish, it wasn't intentional," he said, looking anything but sincere.

"Right," she said, tossing her napkin onto the table.

He hid a chuckle behind a cough. "So Gus doesn't like your fiancé."

"Gus doesn't like any man who can't ride a horse." She stood, gathering her empty plate and silverware. Leaning across the table, she reached for Tyler's plate. "He wants me to marry a cowboy."

She nearly dropped the plate, when Tyler's big hand covered hers. "Maybe your daddy's got a point. There's something to say about cowboys."

"There's a lot I could say about cowboys," she said, struggling to keep her voice even. Her heart was pounding so hard, she was afraid Tyler would hear it. "None of which is acceptable enough to mention in polite company."

"What'cha got against cowboys, Skye?" he asked, his tone soft but deadly.

"How much time do you have?" she returned, tugging her hand, trying her best to slip away.

"I've got all night." His grip tightened. He pulled her closer.

Despite the heat, a shiver traveled down her spine. "I don't trust 'em," she said in a rush, wishing the words hadn't sounded quite so desperate. "They make promises they don't intend to keep."

"I've never lied to you, Skye," he whispered. With his free hand, he took the plates from her trembling fingers, setting them safely down on the table.

She swallowed hard. "Cowboys don't stay put for more than a minute."

"I'm not going anywhere."

"Only because you're not able. You've got a bull to thank for making you a homebody."

He shrugged, giving a boyish grin. "Maybe you're right."

Skye studied him warily, considering her options. Flight or fight? Tyler's run-in with the bull had left him in a weakened state. He wasn't in any shape to do her real harm.

Or was he?

Dinner on the patio had gone better than she'd expected. Tyler appeared to have gotten a second wind. He certainly seemed to have worked up quite an appetite.

Only, she didn't intend to be served up as dessert.

"Tyler, I think it's time to call it an evening," she said firmly.

"What's your rush?" he asked, twining his fingers with hers. "The night's still young."

"And I'm getting older and wiser by the minute." She gave her hand another tug, harder this time.

For someone who professed to have an injured back, he certainly hadn't lost any of his muscle tone. Tyler held on tight to her wrist, using the momentum of her fruitless efforts to escape to throw her off balance. Before she had a chance to stop it, she felt herself tumbling forward.

He gave a little grunt—of pain or pleasure, she wasn't sure which—as she landed across his lap. Struggling against his overwhelmingly male strength, she opened her mouth to protest.

And Tyler took advantage.

He lowered his mouth to hers, quieting her with a kiss.

Chapter Six

Skye tasted like sweetness and warmth, all wrapped into one. Her lips were soft, trembling when Tyler gently took them. Feathering a kiss, he teased her, tested her for willingness. Finding no resistance, he deepened his exploration.

She shifted against him, her elbow grazing his sore ribs. The pain was noticeable, but not enough to stop him. There were some things in life that were worth a price. Getting the chance to kiss Skye again was one of those things.

Since the chaste peck they'd shared at the rodeo, he'd dreamt of repeating the pleasure. Unlike the last time, however, this would not be an innocent kiss. This time, there was no one watching, no one to stop them. No one but themselves to set the limits.

He brushed his tongue against her lips and found willing entry. Stifling a moan of ecstasy, he delved into the sweet heat of her mouth.

Gasping—in what he hoped was delight—Skye brought

a hand to his face. At first, he thought she was going to slap him away. Instead, she smoothed the tips of her fingers against the sandpapery roughness of his beard.

Tiny jolts of awareness sparked deep inside him, sending a sensual current of electricity traveling all the way to the pit of his belly. He felt himself harden at her touch. Snuggling her more securely on his lap, with the heel of his boot, he pushed the chair back a couple of inches from the table, giving them more room to manuever.

The move cost him.

Pain ricocheted up and down his injured spine. He clamped his muscles against the throbbing ache, releasing an involuntary breath of surprise.

Skye stiffened in his embrace. She pushed away, ending the kiss.

"Hey, now," he said, forcing a smile, not wanting the moment to end. "Where do you think you're going?"

Taking it slow and easy, he wove his fingers through the silky strands of her hair, holding her secure. Careful not to jar his back, he used the strength of his arms to pull her closer. Once she was where he wanted, he nuzzled her earlobe with his lips, struggling to recapture the romantic mood.

"Tyler, Tyler, Tyler," she whispered—in admonishment or bliss he couldn't tell. With a sigh, she closed her eyes and tilted her head back, allowing him access to her neck.

He availed himself of the opportunity, sampling her smooth skin.

She shivered in his arms.

Tyler hesitated, considering his next move.

Sitting in a chair built for one wasn't going to get him what he wanted. Oh, no. What he wanted was to run his hands along her smooth skin...all of her skin. He wanted a place to stretch out, to feel her warm curves against his hard body. He wanted enough room to make the earth shift beneath them.

If he were in better shape, he'd sweep her into his arms and carry her to his bed. As it was, he'd be lucky if he could hobble to the bedroom without using her as his crutch. Once there, who knew if his back would cooperate and let him enjoy the moment the way he intended. Back spasms had a way of putting a damper on the height of passion.

Sensing a change in his mood, Skye took advantage of his uncertainty. Before he could stop her, she slipped out of his arms and scrambled to her feet. With her hands on her hips, she stood before him. She wore whisker burns on her face and her neck, wherever his beard had chafed her skin. Her breasts rose and fell with each ragged breath she drew. Her expression was one of confused annoyance. He'd never seen her look quite so beautiful.

"What's the matter with you, Tyler?" she demanded. "Are you trying to kill yourself?"

Tyler didn't answer. He found it interesting that the first thing out of her mouth was concern for his welfare, not disapproval at his kissing a supposedly engaged woman.

"You've got a bad back," she scolded, shaking her head in disapproval. "You're supposed to be taking it easy, not testing your sexual prowess."

Without the warmth of her body, the night felt cold, unfriendly, putting him in an ornery mood. He leaned back in his chair, careful not to wince in discomfort. "Funny, I didn't hear you complaining about my back before."

"You didn't give me a chance."

"Come on, Skye," he said, smiling, assuming his most

persuasive voice. "Don't be mad. We were just starting to enjoy ourselves."

"Speak for yourself, Tyler Bradshaw," she said, though her breathless tone belied the protest. She raised her chin in stubborn defiance. "All I have to say is, if you're strong enough to make a pass, then you're strong enough to put yourself to bed."

With that, she gathered up the empty dinner plates, turned on her heel and stomped back to the house. She walked with her head held high, her shoulders straight. The quick swing of her hips kept time to the angry fall of her footsteps.

Obviously, Skye was not a happy filly.

He flinched as the kitchen door slammed shut on its frame. Hopefully, she wouldn't lock the door behind her. He didn't relish the idea of spending the night camped outside on this chair.

Tyler considered his options.

Despite her protests, he knew she was interested. He'd felt the tremors in her body when he'd held her, the quickening of her pulse when he'd nuzzled her neck, and the willingness with which she gave herself when he'd kissed her.

Under normal circumstances, he'd be more persistent.

But these weren't normal circumstances.

And this was Skye. He didn't care what kind of grown-up, womanly body she was masquerading in, she was still the young girl from his past. An affair between them would be too messy. He liked things nice and neat. When an affair was over, he wanted to walk away without a second thought.

With Skye, he had a feeling it wouldn't be so easy.

The sounds of the night—the whir of the bugs, the distant howl of a wild animal and Skye in the kitchen rattling

dishes at the sink—surrounded him. A soft breeze continued to cool his passion-heated skin. He breathed deeply
and inhaled the lingering scent of Skye's perfume.

Fighting temptation, he gripped the arms of the
wrought-iron chair. It was nice outside tonight, he tried to
convince himself, settling himself in for the long haul.

A good night just to sit and think for a while.

Early rays of sunlight stretched across the living room,
waking her from an uneasy sleep. Skye shifted in her
makeshift bed on the couch. She stretched her arms over
her head and yawned widely.

It had been late before she'd fallen asleep. She'd spent
half the night listening for sounds of Tyler. The stubborn
man had remained outside on the patio for over an hour
before coming in for the night. She'd washed the dishes
and was safely in the dining room, under the guise of
concentrating on her thesis—while trying to decide
whether to go outside to fetch him—when he'd banged
open the back door and shuffled down the hall to his
room.

It had taken all of her willpower not to follow him.

Thoughts of Tyler kept her restless the remainder of the
night. She gave up on her paperwork, calling it an early
evening and heading for bed. But she'd ended up tossing
and turning, unable to relax, unable to think of little else
but the kiss they'd shared.

She still didn't understand how she had allowed it to
happen.

Sighing, she told herself some things were better left a
mystery. Such as, why in the world she hadn't said no,
when Tyler had first kissed her? Or why, when she was
obviously in much better shape, hadn't she simply extri-

cated herself from his embrace, and told him no? And last, but not least, why had she enjoyed herself so much?

She pressed a fisted hand to her forehead, trying her best to squeeze the memories from her mind. Thinking about Tyler only made her more confused. Not to mention, it gave her a headache.

Skye pushed herself out of bed. Grabbing a pair of jeans and a T-shirt, she tiptoed to the bathroom and dressed quickly for the day. Tyler's bedroom was quiet when she passed by. Unbidden, a picture of Tyler asleep in his bed formed in her mind. She swallowed hard at the erotic images that followed. Steeling herself against temptation, she hurried down the hall. She picked up her cowboy boots in the kitchen and slipped quietly out the back door.

Plunking herself down on the top step of the porch, she squirmed her feet into the boots, breathing deeply the fresh scent of dawn. The morning sky was clear and bright, promising another Texas scorcher. The first light felt warm against her arms. Since the sun hadn't gotten a firm foothold in the sky, as of yet, the temperature was still bearable.

Boots on, she clambered off the porch and headed for the horse barn.

The red barn was big, dark and intimidating, reminding her of the first time she'd seen the ranch. She'd been five years old and scared to death because she knew that she was being handed over to her grandmother since her daddy didn't want her anymore. Blinking back the memories, Skye allowed her eyes to slowly adjust to the darkness. Narrow slats of sunshine angled in through the aging siding. Dust motes floated in the air. The scrape of a pitchfork told her she wasn't alone. Jack, Gus's ranch hand, was already at work, cleaning out the stalls.

"Mornin', Skye," he called out to her, a grin splitting his narrow face. Jack was a short man with a wiry build. He looked more like an ex-jockey than a rodeo man. In his day, however, he'd held his own against the wild broncos. He'd been a champion rider many times over. "How are you today, honey?"

"Couldn't be better," she lied. She toed the dirt floor, kicking up a cloud of dust, letting her insecurities peek through. "Jack, if it isn't too much trouble, I'd like to…to ride one of Gus's horses."

"Trouble? Don't be silly. You'd be doing me a favor." He took off his cowboy hat and scratched what little was left of his gray hair. "Which horse would you like to try? Scout's the gentlest, he'll give you an easy first ride. But now, if you're feeling a little frisky, Lobo's your man. He'll keep you on your toes."

Just what she needed. Another man in her life to keep her off guard. "No, that's okay. I think Scout will be fine."

"Sure thing." Jack leaned the pitchfork against the rails of an empty stall. Striding down the aisle, he spoke as he went, "Scout's a good ol' boy. He'll take good care of you. All you have to do is point him in the right direction and he'll make sure you get home safe."

Skye followed at a slower pace. Unexplainably, Scout sounded as though he shared the same qualities as Ralph, her fiancé. Goodness, honesty, reliability—all very commendable attributes. She frowned. So why did it feel as though she were taking the safe bet…with the horse, as well as with the man?

Jack opened the stall and drew out a handsome, chestnut gelding. With a soothing voice, he slipped the bridle and saddle into place. Scout's ears moved back and forth, as though he was trying to catch each and every soft-spoken word from Jack. Even when he tightened the girth around Scout's belly, the horse didn't shy away.

Gus had told her that Jack had a way with horses. It was as though they understood him—or he, them. No matter which, Skye envied his carefree handling of the horse, wishing she had half as much confidence when it came to the male animal.

Jack patted Scout's mane. "He's all ready for you. Need some help up?"

She shook her head. "I think I still remember how to do it. But stick around, just in case I forget."

With Jack holding on to the bridle, Skye put her foot into the stirrup.

Scout shifted against her weight, but Jack calmed him with a soothing, "Whoa there, boy."

Using the saddle horn for leverage, she hauled herself up and swung her leg over. With a victorious smile, she found the other stirrup and settled herself onto the saddle.

"See now, you didn't forget," Jack said, giving her a toothy grin of encouragement. "You'll be fine."

"So far, so good," she admitted, trying not to be too pleased with herself. The horse wasn't moving yet. When he did, the real test would be whether or not she could stay in the saddle.

She gathered the reins and nudged the horse forward with a gentle squeeze of her thighs. Scout responded a little quicker than Skye expected, throwing her off balance for a moment. Just like most men she'd known in her life, she told herself, rolling her eyes. Quickly, she righted herself and guided the horse outside into the fresh, morning air.

For the next forty-five minutes, she allowed Scout to reaquaint her with the ranch that had been her home for almost twenty years. At an easy, walking gait, they followed the fencerows, testing the boundaries of the property. Feeling more confident, she let Scout pick up speed to a slow canter and veered off to the right to find a creek that Skye remembered from childhood.

Once there, she slid off of Scout's back, giving her tender muscles a chance to recover. While the horse had his bit of refreshment, Skye looked on with a melancholy eye. The creek was smaller than she'd remembered, little more than a big puddle. But there were still rocks to climb, trees for shade and plenty of room for daydreams. It wasn't any wonder why this had been her hideaway when life seemed too difficult to understand. Here, no problem seemed too big.

Not even a problem the size of Tyler Bradshaw.

"Time to go, Scout," she said, reaching a soothing hand to the gelding. As though sensing that she was a novice, the horse took extra care to hold still as she remounted him. She patted his neck, thanking him for being kind, and whispered, "Take me home, boy."

He readily complied.

Skye gave the horse free rein to gallop home, slowing him down as they came within sight of the barn. With the wind in her hair and the sun on her face, her heart felt lighter than it had in months. She could almost believe she hadn't a care in the world.

Until she spotted Tyler standing at the gate of the paddock, waiting for her.

Somehow, he had made it out to the stables on his own. The stubborn man was leaning so hard against the fence it was a wonder either of them were still standing. With an unnerving intensity, he watched as she rode into the yard.

The inner calm she'd only just achieved vanished in a haze of confusion and steamy awareness. She thought she'd have more time before facing him again. The problems she'd just cleared from her mind returned with a vengeance.

She blamed Tyler for her relapse.

Determined not to let her discomfort show, she slowed Scout to a stop in front of him. "How'd you get out here, Tyler?"

"I walked," he said in a flat, unfriendly voice.

Skye felt an irrational upsurge of irritation. After what had transpired between them last night, she expected a more cordial greeting. Or, perhaps, it was what *hadn't* transpired between them that was putting him in such a bad mood.

She scowled. What did he have to be so moody about? She was the one who should be angry. After all, he was the one who'd made an unwanted pass. Not her.

A sharp retort rested on the tip of her tongue, but the heat of her anger died when she took a closer look at Tyler. His face was pale. Sweat beaded his forehead. His jaw was clenched against obvious pain. Tyler didn't look like a man who needed any more misery heaped onto his shoulders.

Jack sauntered out of the barn to join them. "How was your ride, Skye?"

"Wonderful," she admitted, slipping effortlessly off the horse.

Feeling the intensity of Tyler's unwavering gaze, uneasily she handed the horse over to Jack. Instinctively, she knew there was more to Tyler's study than mere appreciation of the female body. There was a touch of envy in his gaze...a bitterness that seemed out of place.

Tyler had nothing to envy about her riding skills. She was as rusty as one of those ol' nails holding together the horse barn. Something else was bothering him.

If it wasn't about her, then it had to be him.

The unease which had been dogging her since Tyler arrived on her doorstep turned into a full-blown case of the worries. Tyler wasn't recovering as quickly as she'd expected. She hadn't been privy to his consultation with his doctor, so she didn't know the full extent of his injuries. She suspected they were more serious than she was led to believe. Skye bit the inside of her lip to keep from demanding an explanation.

What wasn't he telling her?

"Skye," Tyler said, breaking into her troubled thoughts.

Startled, she looked up at him with a guilty blush warming her cheeks. She wondered if he could read her mind, if he knew she was thinking about him.

An embarrassed expression flitted across his face. Grimacing, he averted his eyes and said, "It seems I'm going to need some help getting back to the house. If you wouldn't mind…"

The words faded, but not the knowledge of what the request had cost him. He looked like a man who'd gambled and lost his most precious possession. His pride.

Without another word, Skye went to his side.

Tyler looped an arm across her shoulders and leaned his weight against her.

She took on the burden without complaint. Slowly, quietly, they made their way to the house.

The next time a bull decides to use you as a punchin' bag, you won't be walking away from it—if he doesn't kill you first.

Gus's warning tumbled about in Tyler's mind.

Mr. Bradshaw, the extent of your back injury is worse

than I'd expected. Only time will tell if you'll be able to ride again.

Tyler squeezed his eyes shut, trying to block out the doctor's unwanted prognosis. Lying in bed, with the curtains drawn against the intense afternoon sun, he struggled to chase the demons of despair from his mind.

The fact that his spinal injury was serious had finally hit home. He had realized that this morning when he'd stepped outside and tried to walk across the yard to the stables. Getting himself to the horse barn had cost him every bit of strength he'd possessed.

Getting himself back to the house had cost him even more.

It had cost him his pride.

Not that Skye had reveled in his humiliation. Quite the contrary, she'd been unusually quiet. No "I told you so's." No "Tyler, how could you be so stupid?" None of her normal tidbits of sage advice. It was as though she understood how much he was really hurting.

Which made it only worse.

Skye had seen him at his worst. And when she had, she hadn't bolted or abandoned him. She'd stuck by him, helping him with a quiet strength that a man couldn't help but admire.

Which was why he'd spent the rest of the day holed up in his bedroom, licking his wounded pride like an injured animal.

The last thing he wanted was Skye's pity. What he needed was to get his life back to normal. Only, he had a funny feeling that normal was the last thing he was going to get. For the first time since falling off the bull, he forced himself to consider the possibility that he might never be riding again.

Riding bulls, riding horses, riding...period.

The doctor gave him no promises. His career as he knew it might very well be over. Tyler closed his eyes and drew in a steadying breath.

What the hell was he going to do with the rest of his life?

Unable to stop himself, a picture of Skye formed in his mind's eye. He couldn't forget the way she'd looked this morning, riding toward him on that chestnut gelding, with the wind lifting her hair. Her face flushed from the exertion of the ride. Her blue eyes glittering in the morning sunlight. A contented expression on her face.

She'd looked so damned beautiful.

When he saw her, he'd felt such an intense longing to be out there with her, riding right alongside her, that it had hurt to breathe. He didn't know which pained him more, wanting what he couldn't have, or knowing he'd never be able to have it.

A sharp knock sounded at his door.

Two guesses who was coming a callin'. Tyler moaned in frustration. Skye couldn't have picked a worse possible moment for a visit.

"Leave me alone, Skye," he hollered, pulling the covers over his head. "I'm trying to sleep."

"Sorry, Tyler," Skye said, barging into the room. "I can't do that. It's time to get up. We're having guests this evening."

"Guests?" He pushed the covers aside and struggled to sit up. "What are you talking about?"

"Gus is bringing a few friends over for dinner." She strode to the window, pulling open the curtains. Sunlight flooded the room, blinding him. "Your rodeo buddies are all anxious to see how you're doing."

Scowling, he squinted against the light. "I'm in no mood for company."

"That's too bad. They're coming anyway."

"For Pete's sake, Skye." Anger spurred an unexpected surge of energy. Forgetting about his sore back, he swung his legs off the bed, letting his feet hit the floor with a thump. Pain arched along the curve of his spine. He drew in a sharp breath, locked his jaw and cussed his way through the worst of it. Once the pain subsided, he shot her an irate glance. "Couldn't you have asked me first before inviting somebody over?"

She raised a questioning brow. "Would you have agreed?"

"Hell, no."

"There's your answer," she said, smiling sweetly.

He narrowed his eyes. "You really do enjoy torturing me, don't ya?"

"I certainly do, Tyler. I spend my hours dreaming up new ways to get on your nerves. It passes the time when I'm bored."

Tyler raked a hand through his hair. He drew in a slow, calming breath, struggling to keep his temper in check. Soon, very soon, he told himself, his back would be healed. When it was, he'd be taking the quickest route out of this damn ranch. And when he did, Skye Whitman would have one less cowboy to kick around.

Ignoring his obviously foul mood, she stripped the blanket off the bed, tossing it in a heap on the floor. "You're going to have to move, Tyler. I need to change the sheets. You're in my way."

He gave a low growl of frustration. "Do you have to do that now?"

"You've been in this bed for four days straight." She wrinkled her nose, sniffing the air disdainfully. "Do you have to ask?"

Stunned by her bluntness, Tyler's mouth dropped open.

Moments ago, he'd grudgingly admired the gentle kindness she'd shown him earlier this morning. Now there wasn't a touch of sympathy to be found. Now she was being bossy, pushy and rude. In the course of a few hours, she'd gone from Florence Nightingale to Attila the Hun. What the hell was going on here?

Taking his silence for an answer, she continued, "Speaking of cleaning up, you could use a good scrubbing yourself. How about if we get you into the bathtub, Tyler? You want to look presentable tonight, don't you?"

Presentable? As in, he wasn't? Anger got the best of him once again. He lurched to his feet, ignoring the warning pains shooting down his spine. "Now look here, Skye—" He stopped mid-sentence, the jab at his ego forgotten as the rest of her statement finally registered. "What the hell do you mean *we?* Are you planning on joining me in that bathtub?"

She had the grace to blush. "Of course not, Tyler. Don't be silly. All I meant was…"

"Yes," he prompted, feeling an inexcusable pleasure at her discomfort.

She cleared her throat. "What I meant was if you needed help—" She stopped, bit her lip, not looking pleased with that explanation, either.

"And if I did?" He looked at her, giving her a nod of encouragement.

"I'd do what I could, okay?" Her flush deepened.

Tyler bit back a grin. A person could only let a fish dangle for so long before he felt guilty about making it squirm. He decided it was time to cut the bait.

Heaving an exaggerated sigh, Tyler said, "You don't have to treat me like some invalid, Skye. Fill the damned tub with water. But leave the bath to me. I'll get myself in and out just fine without you."

* * *

He'll be fine, she told herself, straightening the clean sheets on Tyler's bed. He said it himself. He didn't need her help. Picking up a fresh-smelling quilt, she shook out the folds and let it drift open across the bed.

Tyler didn't need anyone's help.

He was a loner. A rodeo bull rider who called the road his home and was damned proud of his independent state. She was lucky he didn't want her getting too close. The last thing she needed to do was start caring about a cowboy.

She didn't...care, that is.

The only thing she wanted was to get Tyler back on his feet. The sooner he recovered, the sooner he'd be out of her life.

Which was why she'd called Gus, of course. It wasn't out of concern for Tyler. What difference did it make to her if he refused to eat breakfast and lunch? Or, after coming in from the stables this morning, that he'd closed the door to his room and wouldn't let her in? For all she cared, Tyler could hibernate in this room until next March.

But she needed the space. She was getting tired of sleeping on the couch.

She smoothed a hand across the quilt. It was a wedding ring pattern, a favorite of her grandmother's. She'd used it often on this very bed. Though, somehow, Skye doubted if Tyler would appreciate the sentimentality.

Tyler. The box springs sighed beneath her weight as she sat down on the edge of the bed. She tapped her foot on the floor and glanced at her watch. Tyler had been in the bathtub for nearly an hour.

What if he'd slipped in the tub and drowned?

The thought brought her to her feet. After the catastro-

phe that first day—Tyler's passing out in the bathroom—
she'd been leery of letting him take too many risks. Since
then, she'd kept a discreet, but constant eye on him. Now,
except for the occasional splash of water, there wasn't a
peep coming from the bathroom. It didn't feel right, leaving him on his own for so long.

Skye tiptoed into the hallway. Leaning against the bathroom door, she pressed an ear to the wood panel. And
heard nothing.

"Dang," Skye muttered. "Maybe he did drown, after
all."

The words were barely out of her mouth when the door
flew open, catching her unaware. Her weight still balanced
against the door, she fell forward...right into Tyler's
arms.

Chapter Seven

Having Skye fall into his arms was a dream come true. Wearing only a towel knotted around his waist seemed...well, convenient, if nothing else.

"Tyler," she gasped, trying to push herself upright.

The effort might have worked, if she hadn't rested her hands against his bare chest to accomplish the feat. His skin sizzled at the contact. Tyler sucked in a quick breath and willed his body to behave.

He failed miserably. The long soak in the hot tub had had the euphoric effect of easing the painful spasms in his back, not to mention, weakening his self-control. Skye looked up at him, her big blue eyes wide and uncertain. He swore that if she said a single word of discouragement, he would have let her go in a heartbeat.

But she didn't.

So, he didn't.

Instead, he pulled her snug against him, making sure she knew exactly what sort of trouble she was getting herself into. As it was, she didn't spit in his face in disgust, or even seem the least bit frightened at the prospect of close contact with an aroused man. He almost wished she had. Cursing the fates that had brought them together, and his own lack of willpower, he claimed her lips in a hungry kiss.

Skye responded with a breathy little sigh. She curled her fingers into the matting of blond hair on his chest. Then, hammering the final nail on the demise of his willpower, she went limp in his arms, pressing her soft body against his.

Tyler moaned aloud and did the only thing that a somewhat healthy, red-blooded man could possibly do at a moment like this. He deepened the kiss. Running his fingers down her body, he traced the curve of her waist and the flare of her hips, before settling both hands firmly on her derriere.

He was a fool, of course.

He'd spent the last hour soaking in the tub, telling himself all the reasons why he was better off without a woman like Skye in his life. Number one on that list being that for the better part of his adulthood, he'd been a loner. While he had to admit, life did seem awful quiet at times, he'd been happy enough. He didn't see a reason to change his single status.

The second reason to stay away from Skye: she was engaged to another man. Now, he might not have a highly moral set of standards by which he lived, but he drew the line when it came to married women—including those who were practically hitched. Risking his life and limb against an ornery bull seemed less dangerous than taking on an irate husband or fiancé.

Not that Ralph—Skye's bookworm of an intended— sounded like much of a threat.

Third, and probably most important on the list, he and

Skye didn't have a whole lot in common. Skye was a scholar, getting her master's degree in philosophy. He'd finished high school by earning his general equivalency diploma. She had domesticity stamped across that pretty little forehead of hers. He lived his life traveling on the road from one rodeo to the next. She'd spent the last six years in Boston, rubbing elbows with the rich and refined. He was a country boy. A Texas cowboy born and bred. A Texan he intended to stay. He'd be leaving his home state only one way...boots first.

This last thought served its purpose, cooling his libido. Gus's formidable image floated through his mind. If Skye's daddy found out that he'd been taking advantage of Skye's generosity, Tyler would be meeting his maker sooner than planned. Reluctantly, he disentangled himself from her arms and ended the embrace.

Skye blinked, looking surprised, and more than a little dizzy.

Placing his hands on her shoulders, he held her steady until she fully recovered her equilibrium. As he waited, he watched her warily, not sure what her next reaction might be. An angry Skye taking a swing at his newly shaven jaw wouldn't surprise him a bit.

He cleared his throat. "You okay, Skye?"

"I'm fine," she said, her voice oddly calm and collected. She brushed away a dark strand of hair that had fallen across her eyes. "Just fine."

He frowned, feeling understandably disappointed. The kiss they'd shared had been earthshaking, a 9.0 on the Richter scale of ground rattlers. Why, his heart was still jackhammering in his chest. His blood was still hot and pulsing with a lusty need. His body still ached with wanting her. The kiss certainly deserved more of a reaction than...just fine.

He narrowed a glance. "That's all you have to say?"

She bit her lip, considering an answer. Finally, she shrugged and said, "Dinner's in less than an hour." Scanning his towel-clad body from head to toe with a critical eye, she added, "I'd suggest you be wearing a pair of pants when you greet my daddy."

With that she left him standing in the middle of the hall all by himself, letting him cool his heels with an icy slap of rejection.

"Swear to God, this is a true story," Slim Meyers, one of Gus's cronies, declared. The antithesis of his nickname, Slim was a big man with a round face. He had shoulders wide enough to stop a freight train and a beer belly that hung over his belt. Holding up both of his beefy hands in the air as though he were taking a double oath, he continued his tale. "It happened last summer in Odessa. Tyler was riding on this bull named Shorty. Now, they called him Shorty because of his short little legs. Hell, if Tyler'd stretched any during the ride, he'd have been dragging his feet on the ground."

Snickers of amusement sounded across Skye's living room. Six hours after her encounter with Tyler in the hallway, Skye found her house filled with the bulky bodies and rich voices of cowboys.

Reclining comfortably against the cushions of the couch, Tyler shook his head, looking half amused, half embarrassed by his friend's tale.

Taking her place on the opposite side of the room near the fireplace, Skye couldn't help but smile. She'd taken a risk inviting Tyler's friends to the ranch. As moody as the stubborn man had been lately, Tyler could have spent the evening locked up in his bedroom, refusing to come out. But he hadn't. Instead, he'd bit the bullet and rejoined the land of the living long enough for an evening with the boys.

In an attempt to cheer Tyler up, shortly after a dinner of barbecued ribs, corn on the cob and apple pie, his friends had struck up an impromptu roast of their own. For the last few hours, they'd been trying to outdo each other with tales of Tyler's escapades on the rodeo circuit.

None of which she was certain she should believe.

"Well, halfways through the ride, Shorty tuckers out," Slim continued, breaking into her thoughts. He gave a wink. "I guess ol' Tyler was too much for him. Anyways, this bull up and stops…just quits movin'." He hooted with laughter, slapping a hand to his wide knee, looking thoroughly tickled by the memory. "If the dang bull wasn't still standing, I'd have thought the animal had died."

The snickers of amusement turned into protests of disbelief.

A flush of color spread across Tyler's face. He rubbed his chin with the knuckles of his hand, looking as though he were trying to stop a grin.

"Billy Bob Hawkins was clowning that night." Slim frowned, scratching his full, bushy beard. "Or was it that Rodriguez kid?"

"Who cares?" Gus bellowed, tossing a beer cap at Slim's ample girth. "Get on with the story."

Scowling, Slim cleared his throat. "Anyways, the clown walks up to the bull, as easy as though he were going to say 'hidy do' to the critter, and kicks him in the a—" Slim stopped and glanced at Skye, smiling weakly. "Pardon my French, Skye—kicks him in the *behind* to get him started again. By that time the buzzer rang and it was too late to do much good. Besides, the dang bull just started trottin' back to the gate like he knew his job was over for the night.''

Gut-hugging howls of laughter erupted across the room.

"I don't believe it," Joey Witherspoon said, wiping tears of mirth from his eyes. "Tell us the truth, Tyler. What really happened?''

Tyler allowed a grin of his own. "Just like Slim said, the bull called it quits in the middle of my ride. The judges disqualified me because of that stupid animal. They called it incomplete.''

Skye clapped a hand over her mouth, nearly laughing aloud as a picture of Tyler arguing a call with the judges formed in her mind. She had firsthand knowledge of just how stubborn he could be. He was a fighter; he wouldn't have given up easily.

Along with the laughter, an unease edged into her light-hearted mood. Her smile faded. If only she could direct a little of that fighting spirit toward his recovery, she'd feel a whole lot better. She pushed the thought from her mind, refusing to allow the evening to be spoiled by brooding.

Goodness, she mused with a sigh, forcing her attention to the room full of cowboys. She'd forgotten just how much she'd enjoyed listening to the stories her father's friends could spin. She'd spent many a night as a child falling asleep to their tall tales. Though she had to admit, entertaining a crew this size was enough to wear out even a grown woman. She smothered a yawn. Not that she'd allow anyone to know that she was tired.

The smile on Tyler's face was worth any price she had to pay.

Besides, after what had happened between her and Tyler this afternoon in the hallway, she wasn't sure if she really wanted to be alone with him just yet. She didn't trust herself not to fall into his arms again.

This time, intentionally.

Her attempt to hide her fatigue didn't go unnoticed. Joey was watching her, frowning his concern. He came to her rescue, making a show of glancing at his watch. "I hate to bust up the party, but it's almost midnight. Time for me to go. Juanita will be worried if I don't get home soon."

Not surprisingly, a round of catcalls filled the room.

"Joey's gotta go home to mama," a teasing voice called out.

"Don't want to make the little lady mad, now, do ya, Joey?" another echoed.

"Juanita can't sleep without her Joey in bed next to her," someone else chimed in.

"Well, boys, at least I've got a warm body to snuggle up to." Joey stood, unfolding his massive body, leaving no doubt in anyone's mind that he could pulverize any cowboy in the room if the mood struck. Despite his size, he took the teasing with an easy grin. "Think about that when you're all alone in those empty beds of yours."

The remark had its desired effect, quieting the rowdy group.

Skye blinked, her gaze traveling across the room in surprise, taking in the petulant faces of the cowboys. It had never occurred to her before that, with the exception of Joey, all of her father's friends were bachelors. Happily so.

No wonder Tyler fit in so well with this group.

The thought unnerved her. Tyler was a cowboy. He wasn't the kind of man to settle down. It was time she remembered that and guarded her heart.

One by one, the cowboys stood, stretching their legs, making their way slowly to the front door.

Mindful of her hostess duties, Skye joined them. Amid

a round of thanks and good-night from the boys, she noticed her father lingering behind. Tyler was still sitting on the couch. Gus had taken up residence on a nearby chair. With a hand on Tyler's shoulder, he spoke to him in a hushed whisper, his expression earnest.

As she watched the pair, the hard-fought smile disappeared from Tyler's face. He listened to her father in stony silence, his jaw set, his eyes narrowed.

Skye bit back a sigh. She knew that look only too well. Whatever Gus was saying to him, Tyler did not like it. After seeing the last of her guests outside, Skye returned to the living room. Surreptitiously, she made her way to the pair, angling for a better position to eavesdrop under the guise of gathering up the empty beer cans.

As she drew near, she caught Gus's end of the conversation, "The appointment's the day after tomorrow—"

"I told you, I'm not going," Tyler said, cutting him off, his scowl almost as sharp as his tone. "We've been through this before, Gus. I can take care of myself. There's nothing more a doctor can tell me that I don't already know."

"That you *don't* know, or that you don't *want* to know?" Gus shot back, meeting Tyler's ferocious glare with one of his own.

Silence strained between them. They stared each other down, their expressions as fierce as a pair of wild stallions struggling with a primal need to dominate. The tension in the room felt oppressive, thick enough to smother.

Setting the beer cans on the coffee table with a clatter, Skye broke the silence. "You know, Tyler, I'm running kind of low on supplies. If you need to go into town, I'd be glad to give you a ride."

"I don't need a ride into town," Tyler said through gritted teeth. Slowly, he turned to face her.

Her bravado melted under the heat of his fiery gaze. She fought the urge to turn and run. Ignoring the goose-flesh prickling her skin, she insisted, "It wouldn't be any trouble, Tyler. Really, I could use the company—"

"Forget it, Skye. You're wasting your time," he broke in sharply.

She flinched.

Seeing her reaction, the anger went out of his eyes. Tyler sighed. He averted his gaze, cursing softly beneath his breath. His voice softened as he tried to make amends, hiding his outburst behind a good ol' boy smile of geniality. "Skye, you couldn't pay me enough to get back in that tin can car of yours."

"Well, hell, if that's the only problem, then you don't have to use her car," Gus said, taking advantage of his weakening anger. "I'll be here at nine o'clock sharp and take both of you into town with my car. I've got enough shock absorbers on my Caddy to make the drive so smooth that you'll think you're floatin' on a cloud."

Tyler's expression hardened. He opened his mouth to protest.

Gus pulled himself to his full six foot three inch height, daring Tyler to argue, quieting him with a single glance.

Skye crossed her arms at her waist, holding her breath, waiting for Tyler's answer. She was uncertain why it was so important to her that Tyler keep his doctor's appointment. In her heart she felt there was more at risk than Tyler's good health. It was as though the balance of his future—of both their futures—rested on his cooperation.

Tyler closed his eyes. He pinched the bridge of his nose between his thumb and forefinger, looking tired and defeated. "I give up. I can't fight both of you."

Skye released her pent-up breath, the tension melting from her muscles.

Gus grinned. "I knew you'd see it my way."

Tyler scowled, looking ready to take up the argument once again.

"I gotta go," Gus said, not giving him the chance. He turned his attention to Skye. Enfolding her in a bear hug, he whispered in her ear, "Don't let that cowboy bother you none. Tyler's just got a lot on his mind. He'll be fine, real soon. You'll see."

His assurances only left her confused and unsettled. She was convinced that there was something more to Tyler's injuries than either one of them was telling her.

Before she could press for an explanation, however, Gus released her. Slipping his cowboy hat low on his head, he headed for the door, calling over his shoulder as he went, "'Night, Skye. 'Night, Tyler. I'll be seeing both of you in a couple of days."

Then he left them.

Without the buffer of Gus's presence, the room felt too empty, too quiet.

Once again, she was alone with Tyler.

Feeling his gaze, slowly she turned to face him.

He hadn't moved from the couch. Before the night was over, she realized, she'd be trying to sleep on that very spot. Undoubtedly, the cushions would still hold the scent of Tyler's aftershave. In her dreams, he would surround her. It would feel as though he were still with her.

None of which boded well for a restful sleep.

"Do you want to tell me what that was all about?" she asked, covering her growing awareness behind an annoyance she didn't really feel.

"No, I don't," he said simply. He pushed against the cushions, preparing himself for an escape.

Skye fought the urge to reach out and help him, knowing any offer of assistance would only heighten his already foul temper. Instead, she watched helplessly as he leaned his weight against the arm of the couch and struggled to his feet. She gave a frustrated sigh. "Tyler, why can't you just talk to me?"

"There's nothing more to say," he insisted, setting his jaw against the pain as he straightened his back and looked at her.

She muttered an unladylike oath beneath her breath. Aloud she said, "Damn you…all you cowboys. You and your stubborn pride."

The words brought a flicker of emotion across Tyler's face. Pain? Anger? She wasn't sure which. The light quickly faded from his eyes. A shadowy mask of indifference slipped into place. In a flat, toneless voice, he said, "Sometimes, Skye, pride is all that a cowboy has left to keep him goin'."

With a show of that cowboy pride, he left her. Slowly, he walked down the hall to his bedroom.

Skye stared after him, keeping up the watch long after the door to his room closed softly behind him.

Two days later, fighting feelings of abandonment, Tyler stood on a hot Dallas sidewalk and watched as Skye slid behind the wheel of Gus's Cadillac. Waves of heat and humidity billowed up from the concrete, making it hard to breathe. She rolled down the window, looking petite and tiny against the roomy background of the Caddy. Her anxious gaze flitted over Gus, before settling upon Tyler.

Her brow furrowed into a frown. "Are you sure you're going to be all right without me?"

No, Tyler told himself, he wasn't going to be all right. The truth was, he didn't want her to go. These last few days, he'd gotten used to having her around. Somehow he'd allowed her to become his rock, a strength to depend

on when his own seemed to escape him. Whatever the
doctors had to tell him, he sure as hell didn't want to face
it without her at his side.

Which was precisely why she had to leave.

Aloud, he said, "Skye, it's only a doctor's appointment.
I'll be seeing you again in a couple of hours."

"You must think I'm silly." Hot color suffused her
face. She gave a self-deprecating smile. "Of course,
you'll be fine. You don't need me. I'd just be in the way."

Her apology made Tyler feel even worse.

Gus leaned an arm against the Caddy, bending down
to speak to Skye. "No offense, honey, but we need to get
movin'. Tyler's going to be late if we don't hurry on
inside."

"That's right, Skye," Tyler said numbly, knowing he
didn't give a damn about being tardy. If it weren't for
Gus dragging him to this doctor's appointment, he
doubted if he'd have shown up at all. "I sure as hell
wouldn't want to be late."

At his bitter tone, Skye's frown deepened. She looked
all the more uncertain.

Tyler could have kicked himself. Of all the people who
knew him, Skye seemed to be able to read him the best.
It wouldn't take much for her to figure out the truth. To
realize just how scared he really was.

Skye sighed. "All right, then. I'll just meet you downstairs in the lobby in a couple of hours."

"Have fun shoppin', honey," Gus said, stepping away
from the car.

Her gaze lingered on Tyler for a second longer, sending
an unwanted heat wave of awareness rippling over him.

Tyler gave a silent moan. He didn't care if he did have
a doctor's appointment, or if Skye's daddy was standing
less than two feet away. If she kept looking at him like

that, he'd be hopping back into that car and suggesting they skip his doctor's appointment and try a new form of physical therapy. One that would never meet with the American Medical Association's seal of approval.

All too soon, she looked away. With a quick goodbye salute, she popped the car into gear. Pulling away from the curve, she merged carefully into the heavy Dallas traffic.

Tyler watched until the big, white Caddy turned left, disappearing around the nearest corner. Sighing, he glanced away to meet the watchful gaze of Skye's daddy.

For a long moment, neither man said a word.

Gus was the first to speak his mind. His voice low and gruff, he said, "You know I've always thought a lot of you, boy." Tyler felt a chill of apprehension run down his spine at the words. "You've been like a son to me."

Tyler swallowed hard at the lump of unease rising in his throat.

"But now..." Gus pointed a finger down the street in the direction Skye's car had disappeared. "Skye's my daughter. And I'd do anything to make sure she stays happy and safe." His friend's pale, blue eyes darkened at the warning. "No matter who's standing in my way."

Discomfiting heat scorched Tyler's face. "Now wait a minute, Gus. You know better—"

"I know what I'm seeing...and I don't like it." Gus released a breath through clenched teeth. "No offense, Tyler. But I've watched you in action too many times. You're quite the ladies' man. There are a string of broken hearts across the southwest to prove it. I don't want my daughter to be one of those unlucky chosen."

Tyler's jaw stiffened. He felt an unexpected anger bubble up inside him, surprising him with its strength. It was on the tip of his tongue to lash out at his old friend, making it clear to Gus that his feelings for Skye were different.

But his own admission stunned him, leaving him speechless.

He'd never felt this way before, this protectiveness, this much caring...not for any other woman.

He wasn't sure if he had the right to feel this way now.

"Gus, you have to know, I'd never do anything to hurt Skye," he said quietly, looking his friend straight in the eye.

"Not intentionally, no."

"You have my promise, Gus," Tyler said, hoping it was a promise he could keep. "Skye's heart, as well as her virtue, is safe with me."

They studied each other for another long moment.

Gus's gaze was steady, assessing.

Tyler's was wary, uncertain. His muscles tensed, instinctively preparing himself for battle. They'd had disagreements before, but nothing quite this serious. Tyler knew if it came to a confrontation with his friend, he wouldn't stand a chance. Gus might be older, but he was in good shape. While on the mend, Tyler knew his back was in no condition to support him in a fistfight.

"I'm holding you to that, boy," Gus said suddenly. The anger melted from his eyes. The lines of tension eased around his face. He nodded his head toward the medical center. "Now, let's get you inside. See what that doctor has to say."

Tyler released a breath that he hadn't even realized he'd been holding. He'd known Gus for a long time. His friendship and respect meant the world to him. Two weeks ago, he wouldn't have considered doing anything to jeopardize those feelings.

Now, he wasn't so sure.

Two weeks ago, Skye hadn't yet drifted back into his life.

Skye circled the block for the second time, debating what she should do next.

There was no sign of Gus or Tyler at the entrance of the building. Which meant they were safely inside the medical center.

Which meant she had two hours to kill.

Dallas was known for its shopping centers. It would be sacriligious to pass up such an opportunity. Unfortunately the last thing she felt like doing was something as frivolous as shopping.

Her heart just wouldn't be in it.

She would be too worried about Tyler to enjoy herself.

She made her decision quickly. Ignoring the blaring horns of protests from fellow drivers, she crossed three lanes of traffic at once and pointed the nose of the Caddy toward the parking garage across the street. Impatiently, she plucked the ticket from the automatic machine and navigated the big car through the entrance barriers.

She climbed three levels of the parking garage before finding a spot large enough to park the oversize car. Her hands shook as she gathered her purse and scrambled out the door. Glancing at her watch, she chose the speed of the stairway over the convenience of the elevator.

Time was running out.

Her footsteps echoed hollowly as they fell against the metal stairway. Her heart kept an erratic beat with each clanging step. Her breath came quick and shallow. She felt the tension build inside her with each passing second.

Once outside, the hot mugginess took her breath away. Skye gasped for air…before starting her mad dash across the busy street. Tires skidded, brakes squealed, horns wailed as she weaved her way through the heavy traffic.

A cool blast from the air conditioner met her at the door of the lobby, raising goose bumps against her flushed skin. Skye glanced at her watch as the minute hand closed on the hour.

It was time for Tyler's appointment to begin.

Breathing a sigh of relief, she settled herself gratefully into one of the cushioned lobby chairs. As silly as it might seem, she'd accomplished what she'd set out to do.

Six floors of office space might separate them, but in her heart she was still with Tyler.

For the last hour and a half, Tyler had been stripped and ogled, poked and prodded, X-rayed and tested, until he found himself gritting his teeth in pure exasperation. There wasn't an inch of his body that the doctor or nurses hadn't had their hands on. Now, sitting on the edge of the examining table with his bare legs dangling over the sides and a cool breeze fanning his backside through the vents of his gown, he watched the unreadable faces of the doctor and his staff and tried to keep a lid on his growing impatience.

Gus sat on a chair in the corner of the room, a smirk of amusement at Tyler's discomfort evident on his craggy face.

"Not good," the doctor said finally. Shaking his head, he stuck a vinyl sheet of X-ray photo onto clips over a clear plastic panel and switched on the light behind it. Tyler was treated to an inside-out view of his spinal cord. The doctor pointed to a spot in the middle of the picture. "See this bulge? For now, that's the worst of your injury, a ruptured disk. It's putting pressure on your nerve endings, causing your pain. As a result, every time you try to move, the muscles of your back spasm involuntarily."

"Okay," Tyler said, slowly digesting the diagnosis. "You know what's wrong, so fix it."

"We can, with the treatment I've already prescribed," the doctor said. "Bedrest, painkillers, anti-inflammatory medicine—"

Tyler shook his head. "I've already told you—"

The doctor held up his hand. "I know, I know...you don't want the painkillers."

"So it's not as bad as you thought, right? That means—" The words stuck in Tyler's throat. He swallowed hard, forcing himself to relax, trying not to get his hopes up too high. "That means I can ride again, right?"

"No, it doesn't. This is just a temporary fix. Not a guarantee for a complete cure." The doctor sighed, as he sat down on an adjustable stool beside the examining table. "Tyler, your spinal cord won't endure another injury. If you keep riding the bulls, you're putting yourself at a high risk for a compression fracture of the spine. Once that happens, we're talking about mandatory surgery, screwing metal rods into your spine and wearing a brace to hold your back in place. After that, it would mean weeks of rehabilitation to get you back on your feet. Even then, you'd run the risk of nerve damage." He narrowed a meaningful glance. "Not to mention, the risk of impotence."

From his spot in the corner, Gus released a slow, whistling breath, muttering an appropriate, "Damn."

Tyler refused to comment, not trusting himself to speak.

The doctor continued, "Riding a bull puts more strain on the vertebrae than it could possibly be expected to handle. It's only a matter of time before something has to give. And give it has." He tapped a finger at the X-ray. "In the form of disks and joints that are plainly worn out."

Tyler felt a chill sweep his body. The urge to turn his back on the doctor, to curl up in a tight ball of denial, was overwhelming. He gripped the edge of the examining table with both hands, steadying himself, waiting for the pounding of his heart to subside.

"Tyler, listen to me carefully. At this point, I'd recommend sticking with the bedrest. Give yourself a little more time to let the swelling go down and then we'll get you into some physical therapy. We can make a more informed judgment on how to proceed after that." He rose to his feet, looking Tyler straight in the eye. "A word of warning, though. Once the swelling's gone down, you're going to start feeling better. Don't fool yourself into thinking you're cured. And for God's sake, stay off of the bulls. Or you'll be setting yourself up for irreparable damage to your spinal cord."

After dropping the grim prognosis onto his lap, the doctor left Tyler to absorb the news and to pick up the pieces of his shattered life.

Gus stood, shifting uncomfortably. Unwanted pity shone in the older man's eyes. Tyler had to look away from the sight. "I'll just leave you to get dressed. I'll be outside...if you need anything."

Tyler nodded, not trusting himself to speak.

The door to the examining room *shushed* as it closed behind Gus. Muffled voices sounded in the hall outside. The stillness of the room crept in around him, threatening to smother him with its weight.

The doctor's words echoed in his mind...*irreparable damage to your spinal cord. For God's sake, stay off of the bulls....*

Stay off the bulls....

Tyler pushed himself from the table, forcing the doctor's words from his mind. He dressed slowly, feeling like an old man before his time. When he finished, he opened the door and found Gus waiting for him in the hall.

"I've already checked you out. We can go on home now."

Home. Tyler almost wanted to laugh. He had no home. He had no career. He had nothing.

The ride down in the elevator was accomplished in silence. Once the silver paneled doors opened, they stepped out into the marbled lobby. A lone figure stood from the bank of chairs off to one side of the big room.

It was Skye.

Tyler's breath caught. His heart skipped a beat at the anxious look in her eyes. It took all of his willpower not to walk over to her and gather her in his arms, losing himself in the reassuring warmth of her embrace.

She forced a smile. "Hey, Tyler. How was your appointment?"

His throat felt dry. He could not answer.

Gus looked at him, his silvering brows drawn into a worried line. "It went okay, honey. About as well as we expected."

"So what did they say?" she pressed, proving herself to be her father's daughter...stubborn.

For the life of him, Tyler still could not find the words to respond. He couldn't admit to Skye what a dismal failure his life had become.

"You're starting to worry me, Tyler," she said with a nervous little laugh. "What did the doctor tell you?"

Meeting her gaze, careful to keep the emotions tumbling about in his mind to himself, he gave a slight shrug and said, "Doctors don't know everything."

Ignoring the anxious exchange of glances between father and daughter, Tyler turned on his heel and headed for the door.

Chapter Eight

"**Y**ou sure you want to help out?" Jack asked, pushing back his cowboy hat, looking at her in wide-eyed confusion. "Mucking out the stalls ain't a job for a little lady like you."

"I'm not mucking out the horse stalls because you won't let me," Skye reminded him, letting the "little lady" remark slide without comment. They weren't in the hallowed halls of academia, after all. They were in the heart of Texas, where "little lady" and "missy" were commonplace terms of endearment.

She leaned a hip against the fence railing of the stall and wiped the perspiration from her brow with the back of her gloved hand. Grinning at the older man, she said, "You're the cleanup crew, Jack. I'm just spreading the straw around when you're finished. I promise, a little manual labor won't kill me."

"You ain't used to the heat," Jack grumbled, shaking his head. He took out a pocketknife and snipped the twine on a fresh bale of straw. Closing the knife with a sharp click, he shot her a stern glance. "You start getting light-headed…you tell me. The last thing I want is to have to call Gus and tell him that I'm responsible for giving you heatstroke."

"I'll be fine, Jack," she assured him, giving his arm a reassuring squeeze. "Believe me, you're doing me a favor. All that paperwork on my thesis was giving me a headache. I needed to get outside, work my muscles, get a little fresh air."

"Fresh air?" Jack harrumphed as he gave the bale of straw a kick, sending up a cloud of dust and grain pollen. "You'll be sneezing until next June before you get all the straw dust out of your nose."

Still muttering his dissatisfaction, he grabbed the wheelbarrow and pushed a load of nature's own fertilizer outside to dispose.

Skye sighed and, once again, picked up her pitchfork. Cantankerous cowboys didn't bother her. She was used to their grumpy mutterings and their foul moods. What she couldn't take, what had finally driven her from her own home, was a cowboy who didn't even bother to cuss when he was feeling down and out.

In the past few days, since Tyler's appointment with his doctor, the house had taken on an almost funereal quality. Tyler spent most of his time alone in his bedroom, avoiding human contact. Whenever he did surface, he was polite, but quiet and distant. His appetite had also taken a nosedive. He was behaving like a man mourning a great loss, only Skye hadn't a clue what, or who, had died.

Any attempts on her part to get him to open up, to talk about what ailed him, were met with an obstinate silence. Skye stabbed the bale of straw with more force than necessary, scattering the golden shafts haphazardly across the stall floor. Lord, but the man was driving her to distraction. To make matters worse, she wasn't getting any work done on her thesis thanks to all the time she spent worrying about the bullheaded cowboy.

No man—except, perhaps, Ralph—deserved that much consideration.

Ralph.

A flush of guilty heat warmed her skin. It pained her to admit that, lately, thoughts of Ralph had become too few and far between. Tyler had taken over her life, invading her dreams and waking moments alike. He'd even taken up residence in some of her most intriguing fantasies. Skye bit her lip, tasting the phantom touch of his kiss. She felt an unwanted longing stir in the pit of her stomach.

Pushing away the confusing feelings, she threw herself into the arduous task of spreading and fluffing the straw across the empty stall. Dust rose in clouds, tickling her nose as she worked. Unused to physical labor, her shoulder and upper arm muscles soon burned from the exertion. Perspiration drenched her body, making dust and bits of straw cling to her skin. She ignored the discomfort, attacking the task with a dogged determination, relieved to finally find a vent for her pent-up frustrations.

"Slow down, Skye." The deep voice sent a cold chill traveling down her sweat-soaked back. She froze, unable to move. "This ain't no contest. The horses aren't going to care when you finish getting their boudoirs ready."

Slowly, she lowered the pitchfork, resting the tines carefully against the ground before turning to find Tyler watching her.

With one boot-clad foot hooked onto the lowest rung of the fence and a pair of strong arms draped across the top railing, he studied her with a look of unabashed amusement. "If I had a camera, I'd take a picture. Nobody's going to believe me when I tell 'em you were out here working the barns.'' His grin deepened, drawing her attention to that tempting mouth of his. She swallowed hard, fighting to control a sudden surge of unwanted desire. ''Hell, Skye, I didn't think you even knew what a pitchfork was, let alone how to use one.''

She should have known. The first smile Tyler cracked in days would have to be at her expense. Feeling a bristling of irritation, she said, ''Nice to see you out of bed, Tyler. How's the back?''

''Better than it has been in days,'' he admitted, his easy grin faltering at the reminder. He looked around, inspecting the empty barn before settling his gaze, once again, upon her. ''The house was gettin' kind of quiet. So I thought I'd come outside to see what happened to ya.''

''As you can see, nothing's happened to *me*,'' she said. Resting one hand firmly on her hip, she shot him a meaningful gaze. ''*I'm* not the one who hides out at the first sign of a problem.''

''Ouch.'' Tyler winced in an exaggerated look of pain. ''I guess I deserved that. I haven't been my usual sociable self lately, now have I?''

''Sociable? Tyler, you've been a real pain in the—'' She stopped, reconsidering the wisdom of antagonizing him.

After all, this was the first time he'd made an effort to initiate a conversation in days. While she wanted to take advantage of the opportunity, if she pushed too hard, he just might return to his lair with only his wounded pride to keep him company.

She shrugged with a nonchalance she didn't really feel. ''Well, you know what I mean.''

''Yeah, I know what you mean.'' He shook his head.

"I guess I'll have to mind my p's and q's from now on, or you'll be champing at the bit to get rid of me."

"I never said—"

He searched her face. "Why haven't you, Skye?"

She frowned. "Haven't I...what?"

"Gotten rid of me. If I'd taken on a houseguest as cantankerous as I am, the fool would have been out on his ear before the first day was out. But you..." He released a sighing breath. The sound whispered against her ears like a velvety stroke against her sensitive skin. "Let's just say your patience with me has gone above and beyond the call of duty."

Because I care about you, you idiot.

The words echoed in her mind, but she couldn't find the courage to say them aloud. Her legs suddenly felt weak. She leaned her weight against the pitchfork, afraid her shaking limbs wouldn't hold her weight. "I don't see the need to kick a man when he's down."

"Is that what you think?" His gaze sharpened. "That I'm down?"

She hesitated, choosing her words carefully. "Tyler, I think you're trying to work your way through a few problems. I also think, if you'd share these problems with someone, maybe they wouldn't seem so bad."

For a long moment, he did not respond. The only sound in the big, empty barn was the thudding of her own heart. She nearly jumped in surprise when he finally spoke. "You're wrong, Skye. There are some problems that are just too big to handle, no matter how many people know about them."

"Tyler—"

He held up a quieting hand. "I'm sorry about being so moody. I promise not to allow the rest of my stay to be quite so miserable for you."

"It hasn't been—"

"Yeah, well, I guess I'd best be going inside." He pushed himself away from the fence. Scanning her body from head to toe, he gave her a wink and a devilish grin, reminding her of the old Tyler. "Don't work too hard, ya hear?"

Before she could answer, he was gone, making his way down the aisle with a slow, careful gait. He stepped outside of the shadowy barn into the brilliant sunlight. With his tawny skin and golden hair, the sunshine suited him. Too soon, he disappeared from her line of vision.

It took all her strength not to follow after him.

At least he was talking again, she told herself. It was a start on his road to recovery.

For now, it would have to do.

Later that evening, rubbing his tired, burning eyes, Tyler glanced at his bedside alarm clock. It was 3 a.m. While his body felt exhausted, he was unable to shut his mind off. The wee hours of the morning loomed before him.

He felt restless, unsettled. Every time he closed his eyes, thoughts of what he was going to do now that his career with the rodeo was supposed to be finished played over and over in his mind. All that thinking...and no solutions.

He felt like a tumbleweed adrift in the desert, being swept aimlessly wherever the wind took him. He had no firm route to follow. Somehow he'd lost his sense of direction...and he didn't know if he'd ever be able to get it back.

A fine sheen of perspiration dampened his skin. Hot and frustrated, Tyler tossed aside the sheet and pushed himself out of bed. His back gave only a token protest at the move, proof that he was on the mend. It wouldn't be long before he wouldn't need to impose on Skye's generosity. Soon, he'd be able to leave the ranch.

The thought left him feeling oddly empty inside.

He'd begun to think of the ranch as home. He had nowhere else to go.

The house felt hot tonight, the air stuffy and close. Wearing only a pair of shorts, he headed for the kitchen. He needed a cool drink to clear his mind. Then, maybe, he'd be able to fall asleep.

For the better part of the evening, he'd listened to the sound of Skye moving around the house. Around midnight, she'd finally settled down. The house had been quiet for hours. Undoubtedly, she would be asleep now. Not wanting to disturb her, he tiptoed down the hall to the kitchen, his bare feet padding softly against the wooden floor.

Halfway down the hall, he noticed that the light in the dining room was on.

Tyler froze, unable to move. He thought he was safe, that Skye would be asleep. As keyed up as his emotions felt tonight, he wasn't sure if he was up to facing her. He didn't trust himself to keep his distance. One look into her big eyes, and he wouldn't be able to help himself. He'd be confessing all his sordid little problems.

He listened in the hall, straining to hear the sounds of Skye's movements. He heard nothing. Curiosity got the better of his judgment. Slowly, quietly, he tiptoed toward the dining room.

She was asleep at the table.

With books and papers stacked around her, she'd fallen asleep, one arm crooked under her head on the tabletop, one leg curled beneath her on the chair. Her strawberry-colored lips were parted slightly. He could hear the quiet inhalations of her breaths. The lines of her face were relaxed in slumber. Her skin looked so smooth, his fingers itched to reach out and test its softness.

Asleep or awake, he'd never seen a woman quite so beautiful as Skye.

He indulged himself of this unguarded moment, committing to memory all the details which made her special. The creamy richness of her complexion. The silky darkness of her hair. The compact curves of her petite body, undisguised by her oversize T-shirt.

He wished he could take a picture of this stolen moment, frame it, and store it in his mind's eye for an eternity. Though he doubted if it would be necessary. He'd never be able to forget a minute of the time he'd spent with Skye.

These past days would always hold a special place in his heart.

She stirred in her sleep. A frown marred her forehead. Her eyelids fluttered. She licked her lips, as though she were as thirsty as he felt.

Tyler held his breath, half hoping, half regretting that she would awaken.

With a sigh, she settled down. Her breathing returned to its slow, restful pace. The worry lines eased and she slept the sleep of innocence.

She must be exhausted.

He couldn't leave her asleep at the dining room table. She'd be stiff and sore in the morning. And yet, he couldn't bring himself to wake her.

It wouldn't take much, a single touch, and he'd be lost. He didn't trust himself not to pull her into his arms and make sweet love to her. That was what the man in him wanted. The reckless side of him, the part that didn't care about emotions and consequences.

Another part of him, the part of him that cared more

than he wanted to admit, hadn't allowed him to touch her since the night Gus and his friends had joined them for dinner. The reason was simple. He had no home, no job, no future. Until his life was settled, he had nothing to offer Skye but a single night of ecstasy.

And she deserved so much more.

Bracing himself against temptation, he went slowly to her side. His joints protested as he knelt on one knee beside her. This close, the powdery scent of her perfume teased his nostrils. He could see the rise and fall of her breasts with each breath she took. He wanted to touch the smooth length of her thighs peeking out beneath the hem of her nightshirt.

Curling his hands into tight fists of restraint, he inhaled sharply, cursing his lack of self-control. When he felt his strength return, he reached a hand and gently shook her shoulder. Keeping his voice soft and low, he whispered a quiet, "Skye."

Her eyes blinked open, her expression startled. "Tyler?" She lifted her head, wincing as she brought a hand to her neck to massage the stiffness. "What are you doing up? I thought you went to bed hours ago."

"I did," he said, almost smiling at her sleepy-eyed confusion. "But I couldn't sleep."

She covered a yawn with the back of one slender hand. "What time is it?"

"Three o'clock."

"In the morning? No, it can't be." She frowned. "I just started working on my paper a minute ago—"

"And fell asleep from the looks of it," he finished for her. Admonishing her gently, he added, "You overdid it this morning, helping Jack outside."

"I guess I did." Flexing her slender shoulders, she gave

him a self-deprecating smile. "I've got the sore muscles to prove it."

Tyler grinned, allowing himself a moment too long to gaze into her eyes. And felt a pull of longing that nearly rocked him with its intensity. His breath caught. A sudden tension sizzled in the air. The urge to pull her into his arms nearly overwhelmed him.

As though sensing his battle for control, Skye's smile faltered. But she didn't move away. Instead, she watched him with such wide-eyed expectation that his heart pounded in his chest.

In that moment of hesitation, he knew, with a certainty born of experience, that their need for each other was mutual. It wouldn't take much, just a single touch, to set off a firestorm of desire. All he'd have to do was run his fingers against the smooth skin of her arms, let his hands slide down the length of her body and press her sweet curves against his, and there would be no turning back.

He made his decision quickly. He stood and took a step away, putting much needed distance between them. But not before he saw disappointment flicker in her blue eyes.

"I—um—" He cleared his throat against the strained sound of his voice. "I think you'd better try and get some sleep."

"Yeah, that probably would be a good idea." She averted her gaze, looking embarrassed. Then, as though newly aware of the inadequacy of her attire, she gave the hem of her shirt a tug, vainly trying to cover her thighs.

Tyler wanted to reach out, hold her hands still and stop the self-conscious movements. He wanted to hold her close and tell her how much he needed her. How much he cared for her.

But he couldn't do any of those things.

As long as he had nothing to offer her in return, he

couldn't allow himself to take even a moment of pleasure in her sweet arms.

Before he lost his courage, Tyler forced himself to move away.

"Tyler…"

He stopped, midway to making his escape, then slowly turned to look at her.

She bit her lip, hesitating for a moment. Then, with a slight smile, she said, "I just wanted to tell you good night."

Tyler drew in a deep breath, and released it with a sigh. "Good night, Skye."

Not giving himself a chance to reconsider, he returned to the safety of his own bedroom.

"Skye?"

Startled, Skye jumped as she sorted through a box of research files, almost knocking a stack of papers onto the floor. Embarrassed heat at being caught unaware stung her face as she spun around to find Tyler standing in the doorway of the dining room. Placing a quieting hand on her pounding heart, she said, "Tyler, would you stop sneaking up on me like that?"

He gave an unrepentant grin, his eyes twinkling with mischief. "Sorry, Skye. Next time I'll try stompin' down the hallway with my spurs on. See if you like that better."

In the two weeks since their late night encounter, Tyler's health, as well as his mood, had definitely improved. The bruises on his face had long ago faded. He no longer wore a bandage around his ribs. And, while his movements were still guarded, he no longer walked like a bent old man. It wouldn't be long before the TLC of an old friend would be unnecessary.

Tyler would soon be leaving.

The realization hit like a fist to her stomach. Skye drew
in a steadying breath as she sat down hard in her chair,
trying to understand why the prospect of Tyler's departure
left her feeling so uneasy. She should be thanking her
lucky stars that she would soon be seeing the last of the
demanding cowboy.

But she wasn't. Thankful, that is.

She was going to miss him.

Oblivious to her troubled thoughts, he held out a can
of chili beans in one hand, a box of pasta in the other.
"You've got a choice, chili or spaghetti."

"Chili? Spaghetti?" she repeated, staring at him
dumbly.

"Not much of a selection, huh?" Late afternoon sunlight filtered through the curtains, glinting off his blond
hair. He wore a white T-shirt and a pair of indecently tight
blue jeans. His grin was boyishly sheepish. "It's all I
know how to cook without burning the skillet."

"You're cooking?" she asked, still feeling a little confused, not really sure if she understood him correctly.

They'd fallen into a habit of sharing the evening meal.
The preparation of which, up until now, had been her
exclusive domain. The truth was, it had become a favorite
part of her day. After the dinner was over and the dishes
were cleared, she and Tyler whiled away the hours catching up on the last six years of their lives. She never grew
tired of listening to the Texas twang of his deep voice as
he told her stories of his life on the rodeo circuit.

Though she couldn't help but think that despite the
glory and attention he'd received from being a champion
bull rider he'd led a lonely life on the road.

"I thought I'd give the job a whirl," he said, his voice
bringing her back to the present. He shrugged his wide
shoulders, not looking as confident as he had a moment

ago. "You've been making my meals and taking care of me all these weeks, it's the least I can do to pay you back."

Pay her back? Skye's heart skipped a beat at the finality of his words. Moments ago she'd been wondering how much longer Tyler intended to stay...wondering how she'd ever be able to let him go.

"Tyler, it really isn't necessary." She pushed the chair from the table, struggling to stand on her wobbly legs.

He held both hands up, stopping her. "Now, just sit yourself down. Keep working on that thesis of yours. I can make this meal all by myself."

"Are you sure?"

A chagrined look crossed his face. "Now look, Skye. The meal might not be up to your gourmet standards, but I can guarantee the food will be edible."

Her flush deepened, scorching her cheeks. "I didn't mean to imply—"

"Of course you did." He leaned a shoulder against the door frame and grinned, looking amused by her obvious discomfort. Skye stifled a moan. Despite the platonic bent their relationship had taken these past two weeks, she'd be lying if she didn't admit Tyler was just too handsome for his own good. "Not that I can blame you. I wouldn't trust anything this ol' cowboy had to say, either."

"I never said I didn't trust you, Tyler."

"You never said ya did, though...now did ya?" He watched her, his soft brown eyes studying her face.

Awareness rippled over her. The conversation was taking an entirely too personal turn. She sat stiffly in her chair, fighting the urge to squirm beneath the intensity of his gaze, wondering exactly how she was supposed to answer him.

Evasiveness seemed to be the best course of action.

"Spaghetti sounds good to me," she said, effectively sidestepping the issue at hand, knowing it wasn't really a question of trusting Tyler. Rather, it was a question of trusting herself. "I believe I'm in the mood for Italian tonight. If you need any help, just ask."

Reluctantly, he pushed himself from the door frame. "I don't expect I'll be needing any help. I think I've got everything under control."

Skye wished she could say the same.

With a nod goodbye, looking more fit and agile than she'd seen him in days, he turned toward the kitchen. The heels of his boots echoed solidly against the wooden floor, making her wonder how she'd missed his entrance in the first place. His lean, well-muscled body moved with a familiar ease. There was no sign of stiffness, or a lingering pain in his movements.

Tyler's health was definitely improving.

She wondered just how long it would be before he decided he didn't need her anymore.

He needed Skye now, more than he'd ever needed her before.

Tyler stared in disgust at the mess he'd made in the kitchen. The acrid scent of overcooked hamburger clung to the air. Fat drops of tomato sauce sizzled in the skillet and spat across the stovetop and onto the nearby cabinets. The pot of water holding the spaghetti bubbled and frothed as it boiled out of control.

He didn't know what the hell had come over him, flappin' his gums, braggin' about what a good cook he was. At the moment, he wasn't sure if he could pull this dinner off. Nothing seemed to be going right. The thought of impressing Skye left him feeling clumsy and inept.

If he didn't know better, he'd say he was suffering from a case of the nervous jitters.

But he'd be damned if he'd admit as much to Skye.

"How's everything going, Tyler?" Skye's sweet voice drifted in from the dining room.

Tyler stood straighter, ignoring the dull ache low in his back. "Great," he hollered. "Couldn't be better. It shouldn't be long now."

"Good. I'm famished," she said with a breathy sigh of delight. Despite his strained nerves, Tyler felt his pulse quicken at the sensual sound of her voice. He scowled, irritated with himself. The way his body was behaving, a person would think Skye was moaning in ecstasy, not hunger. Her voice broke into his thoughts. "I'll just get freshened up before dinner."

Holding himself still, he listened to the scrape of her chair against the hardwood floor, the light steps of her feet as they disappeared down the hall, and he felt a moment of panic tighten his chest. *Well, Bradshaw,* he told himself, *time to impress the lady.* Grabbing a fork, he fished a limp strand of spaghetti out of the pot. Blowing on it long enough to make it cool to the touch, Tyler picked up the noodle and threw it against the wall facing the stove.

The spaghetti stuck to the painted white wall.

He nodded, pleased with the results. Perhaps it wasn't a precise method of determining the spaghetti's doneness, but he didn't see the need to knock whatever method worked.

Without thinking, he snatched up the pot of boiling water. Heat stored in the metal handles scorched the palms of his hands. Reacting instinctively, Tyler dropped the pot. A wave of hot water splashed across the stovetop. He jumped back, escaping a well-deserved scalding.

Cursing under his breath, he grabbed a pair of potholders and tried his luck once again. This time, he made it to the sink without spilling a drop. He drained the noodles and plopped them into a waiting bowl. He lifted the skillet off the stove and, giving the sauce one last stir, he poured it over the spaghetti. He left the crusty patches burnt onto the bottom of the pan.

"Can I help?"

At the unexpected sound of her voice, Tyler almost dropped the empty skillet onto his tooled leather boots.

Skye stood at the counter, not two feet away. Her face was flushed, dewy from the heat of the day. The humidity set her dark hair into a riot of curls. She wore a red T-shirt and a pair of faded blue jean shorts, both fitting her like a second skin. He'd never seen her looking more desirable.

He wondered how long she'd been standing there.

Long enough to see what a klutz in the kitchen he really was?

Tyler forced himself to look away from temptation, hiding his awareness behind a quick inspection of the kitchen. In a sweeping gaze, he noted the sauce-splattered cabinets, the spilt water still sizzling on the hot stovetop and the noodle stuck to the wall.

He shot her a sideways glance, raising a brow in question. "How'd ya like to eat outside tonight, Skye?"

"Sounds good to me."

"Well then, grab a couple of plates and we'll eat in style under the stars."

Skye smiled, and Tyler nearly lost his heart.

He forced himself to move away from her. Afraid if he didn't, he'd pull her into his arms and kiss her right then and there. Though he'd wanted to many times over, he hadn't allowed himself to touch her. His life was still as uncertain today as it had been when the doctor had given him "The Bad News." That was how he thought of it, "The Bad News," in capital letters, when the doctor had told him his world as he knew it was over.

He pushed the troubling thoughts from his mind. Juggling the spaghetti and the Parmesan cheese, Tyler led the way to the wrought-iron table and chairs. Lights from the porch lit the table in a soft glow. Heavy vines of sweet smelling flowers draped the trellis that lined one side of the patio, spicing the air with a scent that would always remind him of Skye.

In the mornings, when she thought he was still asleep, he watched from his bedroom window as she puttered about in the yard, coaxing her grandmother's neglected garden back to life. From gardening to horses, life on the ranch suited her. Though he doubted if Skye would ever admit as much to anyone else, including herself.

She seemed almost as determined to leave this ranch, as he was himself.

The clatter of silverware being set on the table snapped him back to the present. Skye was watching him, a curious look on her face.

He cleared his throat. "What would you like to drink?"

"Water would be nice." Frowning, she asked, "Are you sure you don't want me to get it? I'm not used to being waited on."

"Now that's a pity," he said, hiding his sincerity behind a teasing grin. "A woman like you should always have someone wanting to take care of you."

She opened her mouth to speak, probably to protest his hopelessly chauvinistic ways.

But he didn't give her a chance. Instead, he headed back to the house for their drinks, glad for the opportunity to escape. She was so damned beautiful. And he wasn't a strong man. He was used to taking whatever he wanted. Getting through this night without giving in to his desires was going to be a real challenge to his limited self-control.

When he returned, he found Skye leaning back in her chair, her face tilted heavenward. She looked so relaxed, if her eyes weren't wide open, he'd have thought she'd fallen asleep.

"I'm going to miss the night sky the most," she said. Her smile was lazy, contented. "The stars feel closer here on the ranch. Close enough that I could almost touch them if I wanted. They just aren't the same up north."

"There's one way to solve that problem." He placed her water glass on the table and took a seat across from her. She looked at him, a slight frown furrowing her brows. "Don't leave Texas."

She shook her head. "Easier said than done, Tyler."

"Why? I thought you were finishing up your thesis this summer," he said, keeping his voice casual, though his hands were sweating and his heart was thudding against his chest. Wiping his hands on his jean clad legs, he picked a plate and scooped out a generous helping of spaghetti. "That means you'll be out of school soon. What's keeping you from staying?"

"Lots of things."

"You mean, like Ralph?" he asked, passing her the dish of spaghetti. Bringing up the name of Skye's intended was like rubbing salt into a festering wound. Telling himself he was a glutton for punishment, he forced himself to continue. "I guess you're gettin' anxious to head back up North, so you can marry your professor."

She picked up her fork and twirled a strand of spaghetti around it, taking her time to answer. "My life's in Boston now," she said, her voice so soft he could barely hear her. "Not in Texas."

He stared at her for a moment, not trusting himself to speak. If she'd given him a straightforward answer—if she'd said, yes, in no uncertain terms that she intended to marry Ralph Breedlow—he'd have let the matter drop. But she didn't. As far as he could see, it was an open invitation for pressing the point home.

Tyler scooped a helping of spaghetti onto his plate. He dug his fork into the mound of steaming pasta and forced himself to eat. The food tasted like mush. Swallowing hard, he said, "You still have a life in Texas, you know."

"Tyler, I hardly think—"

"People here care about you," he persisted, keeping his voice neutral.

Stopped in midsentence, her mouth closed with a delicate click. She studied him, a curious glint in her blue eyes.

Heat suffused his face. He picked up his glass and gulped down a drink of water to clear away the lump in his throat, before adding, "I know Gus would like for you to stay."

"Gus," she said, shaking her head, looking mildly disappointed. "We've been through this before, Tyler. Gus has gotten along just fine without me all these years. I don't think it would really matter to him one way or another if I stayed, or if I didn't."

"Then you don't know your daddy very well," he said with more force than he'd intended. Unexpected anger bubbled up inside him. "He's a cowboy, Skye. Cowboys don't wear their emotions on their sleeves."

"Maybe they should," she shot back. Her jaw stiffened. She matched his temper with her own. "It would certainly ease the minds of those who cared about them."

The reason for his angry outburst blurred in his mind. At this point, he wasn't sure who he was defending—Gus or himself. "Maybe he just doesn't know how. Maybe he's never felt this way…never cared this much before."

She stared at him, not saying a word.

His heart pounded in his ears as he waited for her to answer. The air felt hot, stifling. Sweat trickled down his back. His grip tightened around the fork, the handle biting into the flesh of his palm. It felt as though his life depended upon her response.

"That's just an excuse," she said finally. She averted her gaze, riveting her attention on her plate of untouched spaghetti. "If someone really cared as much as you say— even a cowboy—he'd find a way to show me."

"Maybe he already has," he said softly.

She lifted her eyes and held his gaze. Her lips parted. She was about to speak.

The toot of a horn interrupted.

Tyler blinked, confused for a moment by the sound. Frowning, he looked down the dusty lane and saw the headlights of, not one, but two pickup trucks. Slowly, understanding dawned. When he'd been injured, he'd left his truck in Dallas. This afternoon, while Skye worked on her thesis, he'd called Joey and Slim and asked them to return it to him.

This evening, he'd been sidetracked by Skye and her beauty and his desire for her. So much so, that he'd forgotten the reason for his treating her to a dinner. He had something important to tell her.

That tomorrow…he'd be leaving.

Chapter Nine

His face tense and drawn, Tyler pushed his chair back and stood.

Skye didn't trust herself to follow. She remained still in her seat and watched numbly as the trucks pulled up alongside them in the yard, kicking up rocks and a cloud of dust with their tires. And she tried not to think what it meant.

She blinked back the unexpected tears that pressed against her eyes. Her heart thudded painfully in her chest with a hollow-sounding beat. She felt empty, drained of all emotion. It was as though she'd fought a battle. A battle she'd come so close to winning. But in the end, she had lost everything.

In her heart, she knew Tyler was leaving her.

Slim slid his ample girth out from behind the wheel of one of the pickup trucks, slamming the door behind him. Joey followed suit in the other. Both men spotted them on the patio and strode over to join them.

Skye forced a smile. "Joey, Slim, this is a surprise. I wasn't expecting you."

Joey shot Tyler a quizzical glance. "Didn't you tell her?"

Tyler looked at her for the first time since the pair's arrival. She drew in a sharp breath at the regret she saw reflected in his eyes. "I—um—asked the boys to bring my truck out."

Slim slapped Tyler on the back. "Tyler says he's feeling better. Fit enough to get back to bustin' bulls."

"Well, maybe not just yet," Tyler said, grimacing in pain...or contriteness, she wasn't sure which. "But I am feeling good enough to take care of myself. It's time I got out of your hair."

"You know you're welcome to stay as long as you like," Skye said, forcing the polite words. All the while knowing her heart was breaking in two.

"I know," Tyler said, his voice whisper soft. "But it's time I moved along, before..."

His voice faded. He left the words unspoken.

Before he did or said anything more he'd regret, she silently finished for him. Unresolved tension filled the air between them.

Joey looked from one to the other, a frown settling across his broad face.

Skye gathered her scattered strength and stood, her legs trembling beneath her. She turned her attention to Joey and Slim. "I'm sure you must be thirsty after that long drive. Would you like a drink?"

Slim smacked his lips. "Why I sure wou—"

Joey nudged the big man, cutting off his answer with a shake of his head. "Thank you anyway, Skye. Slim and I have to get home." He ignored Slim's gaping expression of surprise as he added, "Tyler, give me a call when you get back into town."

Tyler nodded. Shooting a fleeting glance her way, he followed the men to Joey's truck. She watched as they exchanged a few brief words. Then the truck sagged beneath their weight as both men climbed inside, slamming the doors behind them. Tyler stepped back out of the way. The men left as they'd arrived, with a honk of their horn and their tires spitting up a cloud of dust and confusion.

All too soon, she was alone with Tyler.

Rocks crunched beneath his feet as he swiveled around to join her. His eyes never left her face as he walked toward her. She swallowed hard, knowing he must be able to read in her expression the disappointment that she felt.

"Skye, I'm sorry—"

"Sorry for what? For not telling me you were leaving?" She attempted a lighthearted laugh which sounded flat even to her own ears. "You're a guest here, Tyler. You can come and go as freely as you wish."

"Yeah, but I should have said something before—"

"Before," she repeated, once again seeing the regret in his eyes. She forced herself to look away. Dinner still awaited them on the patio table. But, not surprisingly, she'd lost her appetite. "Tyler, I hope you don't mind, but I'm not feeling very hungry right now. I think it would be best if I went inside and tried to get some more work done."

"Of course, I don't mind," he said, his voice hoarse. He sat down hard in his chair, refusing to meet her gaze.

"Thank you for making dinner," she said, feeling the need to soothe him. "It was a nice thought."

"Too bad we didn't get to finish what we started."

She wasn't sure if he'd meant the meal, or the conversation they'd had before Joey and Slim's arrival. His words echoed in her mind, *Maybe a cowboy's never felt this way...never cared this much before.*

It was on the tip of her tongue to ask if it had been himself he'd been speaking of...if he'd meant those words for her.

But she looked at the stubborn set of his jaw, the hard lines of his face and knew it would be pointless. Tyler wasn't the kind of man who would be able to settle down, no matter how much he said he cared. He was a cowboy. It wasn't in his nature to let the dust of one place settle on his boots for long.

She had her own life to live. A life which didn't include Tyler.

Without another word, she hurried back into the safety of the house, chastising herself all the way. Why couldn't she have left well enough alone? Stayed in Boston, lived her safe, but boring, life with Ralph? She should have known better than to fall in love with a cowboy.

They only knew how to break her heart.

Skye awoke to the sound of horses whinnying outside. After her escape from Tyler's presence earlier that evening, she'd worked on her thesis until almost midnight, unwilling to dwell on what was really bothering her. That after tomorrow, she would never see Tyler again. Oh, with their mutual relationship to Gus between them, they'd stumble upon chance encounters. An occasional holiday. A birthday, perhaps. But nothing to compare to the intimacy of these past few weeks.

In her heart, she knew she would never be this close to Tyler again.

Only when she knew he was tucked into his bed for the night did she dare leave the safety of her makeshift office in the dining room. Sleep had eluded her when she'd finally turned off the lights and tried to close her eyes. Tonight, she'd felt each and every lump of the ancient couch. Shifting her weight against the sagging cushions, she'd fought to find a comfortable position.

Finally, exhaustion had won and she'd fallen into a restless sleep.

Now, she blinked the sand from her eyes, squinting at the illuminated hands of the travel alarm sitting on the coffee table. It was two o'clock in the morning. She'd been asleep only an hour at the most.

Tossing aside the lightweight sheet, she padded across the living room to the window. She lifted a corner of the lace curtain and peered outside at the horse barn across the night-darkened yard. All seemed to be in order. Ready to attribute the sound to a case of her overactive imagination, she almost missed the solitary figure standing at the paddock fence.

Even in the shadowy light, she knew it was Tyler.

Clouds chased across the moon, clearing the darkness, casting him in a silvery light. He stood quietly, leaning his weight against the fence, watching as her favorite horse, Scout, high-stepped a dance just for him. Despite the yard that separated them, she saw the haunted expression on Tyler's face.

Tomorrow, he would be leaving.

No matter how many times she told herself it was true, the realization hit her like a blow. She drew in an unsteady breath. Unable to help herself, Skye reached a hand to him, touching her fingertips to the cool pane of the window.

The distance between them seemed unbearable.

Knowing she'd regret her actions later, she followed her instincts and turned from the window. Grabbing the satiny robe that rested on the back of the couch, she pulled it on over her pajamas and hurried from the house. She paused at the front door to gather her flagging courage, then stepped barefoot into the warm night air.

Noiselessly she made her way to the paddock. So absorbed was Tyler in thoughts of his own that her approach went unnoticed. She took the opportunity to study him.

Barefoot, bare-chested, with only a pair of well-worn jeans riding low on his hips, he stole her breath with the primal maleness of his body. If it were possible for a man to be beautiful, Tyler certainly fit the description.

Lean, sinewy muscles rippled across his shoulders, tapering downward to a narrow waist and hips. Long, powerful legs completed the picture. Despite the scars scattered across his body—war wounds from the rodeo, no doubt—he was as close to perfection as she'd ever hope to see.

As though he'd felt the heavy measure of her gaze, he turned to face her. His expression did not change, remaining unnervingly somber. For what seemed like an eternity, he didn't say a word. Instead, he took his turn at studying her, not letting an inch of her body go untouched by his gaze.

Her body quivered with awareness by the time he finally spoke. His voice a husky whisper, he said, "Skye, you shouldn't be out here."

Heedless of his warning, she took a step closer. "I saw you from the window."

"I couldn't sleep," he admitted.

"Neither could I."

"You were earlier, when I left the house."

The implication was clear. Tyler had been watching her while she'd been asleep. The intimacy of his admission shocked her. A delicious warmth flooded her body, pooling low in her stomach. She felt a desire so intense she felt weak beneath its onslaught. Her legs trembled as she closed the gap between them.

A scant few inches away, he towered over her. She stood close enough to feel the radiant heat of his body, to hear the raggedness of his breathing and to trace the strong outline of his powerful chest with her eyes. Yet she felt no danger at his closeness. The only fear that held her was the fear that he would keep a stubborn distance.

Her fears were for naught.

With a low growl sounding deep in his throat, he reached out a hand and brushed the tips of his fingers along the delicate line of her jaw. Then he cupped the back of her neck with his palm and pulled her toward him. Butterflying a kiss against her lips, he raised his free hand to her waist and settled her soft curves snug against his hard body.

The world spun beneath her feet. Skye melted into his embrace. She put her hands on his shoulders and held on tight, afraid if she didn't she'd slide to the ground like a puddle at his feet.

He tore his lips from hers and drew in a sharp breath. She felt the rise and fall of his chest against her breasts. His skin felt hot to the touch, as though there was a fire burning beneath the surface.

He lowered his head, burying his face in her hair, pressing his mouth to her ear. His warm breath sent shivers of desire racing through her as he repeated his earlier warning, "You shouldn't be here, Skye."

"There's no other place I'd rather be."

"You don't know what you're saying."

She pushed away, just far enough so that she could look into his eyes. "I've never been more sure of anything in my life."

He hesitated, then said, "I can't make any promises—"

She brought a finger to his lips, quieting him. "I'm not looking for promises, Tyler. I'm only looking for you."

At first, he didn't answer. He stared at her, his gaze unwavering. And Skye nearly lost herself in the depths of his brown eyes. She held her breath, waiting for him to make the next move.

When he stepped away, she nearly cried out in disappointment. But instead of rejecting her as she'd feared, he reached out a hand, silently asking her to follow.

Without a moment's hesitation, she accepted the invitation.

His big hand swallowed her fingers, warming her with his touch. Quietly, he led her back into the house, and into his bedroom. Leaving the room in darkness, with only the moonlight to show her the way, she followed him to the heart pine bed. There she stood before him, feeling like a schoolgirl waiting for her first kiss.

Nervously, Skye skimmed the room with her gaze, noting the tousled sheets, her grandmother's wedding ring quilt folded neatly at the foot of the bed, and the open duffel bag, half filled with Tyler's clothes, waiting for his departure. In her mind's eye, she tried to picture the room without Tyler in it, and failed. In such a short time, he'd become so much a part of her life, she couldn't imagine her world without him.

Then he touched her.

With slow and deliberate movements, he undid the belt of her robe and pushed it off of her shoulders. The satiny fabric whispered as it slipped to the floor. Her pajamas felt hopelessly flimsy and inadequate, offering little protection against the boldness of his gaze.

But then again, protection wasn't what she wanted from Tyler.

His first kiss was gentle. He tested her, teased her, until

she thought she was about to explode. Then finally, with a brush of his tongue he parted her lips and took what she'd been so willing to offer. With an urgency wrought of desire, he explored the sweetness of her mouth.

All too soon, he ended the embrace.

His eyes never leaving hers, he lowered her onto the bed. The box springs creaked as he lay down beside her. Propped up on one arm, he looked down upon her, then smiled as he lowered his head to her breast.

She gasped as she felt the moist heat of his mouth through the lacy fabric of her pajamas. Impatiently, he lowered the straps and exposed the creamy flesh. Her nipples contracted and hardened as the cool air and his hot gaze caressed her skin. Reflexively, she arched her back as he stroked first one, then the other with his tongue.

The room spun around her. She closed her eyes and buried her fingers in the silky hair at the back of his head. Heat pooled and rippled throughout her body as he suckled at her breast. Sighing, she shifted her leg and brushed her thigh against his hardening body and knew his desire was as great as hers.

In her wildest fantasy, she'd never imagined that anything could feel quite so perfect. She had no regrets, no misgivings at what was happening. Having Tyler make love to her was a dream come true. It was as though they were made to please each other.

Impatiently, she tugged at his hair, lifting his head so she could sample his lips. She kissed him softly, then greedily deepened the embrace, brushing her tongue against his lips, his teeth, plunging into the heat of his mouth. And he followed in kind, taking his turn at giving her pleasure, until it was a game of give and take.

She outlined the strong muscles of his back with the tips of her fingers, hesitating as she stumbled across a scar that spanned the width of her palm. Unexpected tears sprung to her eyes. She gave a soft cry of despair, grieved by the price he'd paid for being a champion bull rider.

He stiffened at the sound, breaking off their embrace to look down at her.

Skye blinked back the emotion, unwilling to let him see her quite so vulnerable. Despite her efforts, a single teardrop escaped from her eyes.

"What's wrong?" he whispered, gently tracing the trail of her tear with his knuckles. His expression shifted, his gaze wary. "Have you changed your mind?"

She shook her head. "No, of course not. It's just—"

"Just what?" he insisted, a frown furrowing his golden brow.

"Your back…all the scars…why do you do that to yourself, Tyler?"

Silence was her only answer. Then with a terse sigh, he rolled back onto the bed, putting an unforgivable distance between them, and said, "You wouldn't understand."

Pulling her pajamas back into place, she sat up in bed and glared at him, feeling an unexpected surge of anger at his dismissive words. "I won't, unless you tell me."

"You know, you're like a dog with a bone," he drawled, laying his Texas twang on thick, looking amused by her persistence. "You just won't let go, will you?"

"A dog?" She raised an indignant brow.

"A pretty one, though," he assured her, smiling that teasing smile of his. He reached out and brushed a dark curl from her face, wrapping it around his finger. "Like a poodle, or one of those little furballs, all tiny and cute."

She frowned, wise to the unexpected resurrection of his "good ol' boy" routine. Whenever Tyler was faced with a problem too great to handle, he tried to joke his way out from beneath its weight. "You're avoiding my question."

He sighed again, louder this time. "That question being…why do I ride the bulls?"

"Tyler—" she growled her impatience.

"You want to know why? Because I'm good at it," he said. His voice took on a clipped, cool tone that seemed out of sync with the warm, loving man she'd held in her arms just moments ago. "Because I can look into the face of a bull and not be afraid. I know I can handle whatever he has to dish out."

She stared at him, uncertain how to answer. Finally, she said, "You should be afraid. When you're not scared, you're not careful. One of these days, a bull's going to kill you."

"Will it matter?" he asked, his easy grin belying the grimness of his words.

She couldn't help herself. Anger at the carelessness with which he'd treated his precious life bubbled up inside her. Acting reflexively, she slapped him across the face, leaving a dark mark on his cheek.

He blinked, looking surprised by her show of emotion. Rubbing the wound gingerly, he chuckled. "You've got a funny way of making love, Skye. I bet you're more than ol' Ralph can handle."

The remark held more of a sting than any physical blow possibly could. She gasped, shocked by the crudeness of his words. Yet at the same time realizing that he was acting instinctively, out of self-preservation. She'd gotten too close. He'd let down his guard and was beginning to care about her.

Tyler might be able to face down a bull, but when it came to showing his emotions he was scared to death.

Knowing this did little to soothe her temper. All that

she could think of was that she was glad he'd decided to make his feelings clear before she'd made the mistake of making love with him. She scrambled from the bed, nearly slipping on her satiny robe on the floor. Picking up the robe, she straightened to find Tyler climbing out of the bed to stop her.

"Skye, I'm sorry," he said, reaching out for her, capturing her hand in his. "Where are you goin'? I didn't mean any harm. I promise not to say another word about you and your professor."

She jerked her hand away, pointing an angry finger at his chest. "My relationship with Ralph is off limits to you."

He took a step back, holding both hands up in mock surrender. "Whatever you want, Skye. Just don't be mad."

It wasn't mention of Ralph that had her up in arms. Long before this evening, she'd had her doubts. Now, the cold, harsh realization that her relationship with Ralph was over swamped her. It didn't take much for her to understand that if Tyler could sway her loyalties from a man she was supposed to love, then that love must not have been strong enough to last in the first place.

But Tyler didn't know of her change of heart. As far as he was concerned, she still planned to marry Ralph. To him, she was just a one-night stand, nothing more.

She was a fool to think otherwise.

"I'm not mad. I'm disappointed," she said, her voice quavering with emotion. "You're supposed to be this brave, strong bull rider. But you're scared, Tyler. So scared that you think that by acting crude, you can push me away. That I won't care about you anymore. Well, congratulations." She gave a sharp, humorless laugh. "You've just won yourself another victory."

Then, knowing she'd said too much, she ran from the room, wondering how she'd ever live down the humiliation of this single night.

Tyler watched her leave with a mixture of disbelief and gut-wrenching fear.

Up until now, he'd lived his life believing that his emotions could be untouched. That if he didn't stay in one place, or with one woman too long, he'd be free from the encumbrances of love and commitment.

But he'd been wrong.

Skye had been waiting in the wings to prove just how wrong he could be.

Tyler sat down hard on the bed, his legs giving out beneath him. He leaned his elbows onto his knees, burying his face in his hands. He felt weak, uncertain for the first time in his adult life. Not since he was a child, waiting for his daddy to come home from a night of drinking at the tavern, had he ever felt so lost, so alone.

When he'd turned seventeen, and had his fill of broken promises from an alcoholic parent, he'd turned his back on the only relationship he'd ever known. At that time, he'd sworn that he would never leave himself vulnerable to the pain of loving and losing ever again.

He should have listened to that child in him, warning him against the hazards of getting too close to anyone else.

The muffled sound of Skye crying in the living room drifted down the hall to his bed.

It took all of his strength not to go to her, to pull her into his arms and tell her just how much he cared. But he couldn't allow himself to do that.

Instead, Tyler lay back on his bed and stared unblinkingly at the ceiling, listening to the sound of a heart that he had broken.

Hearts can be mended, he told himself. Skye still had her Ralph.

She'd soon forget about this ol' cowboy.

The question was, would he ever be able to forget about her?

Tyler glanced around the room, looking for anything he might have left behind...besides his pride, that is. A floorboard creaked in the doorway. He turned to find Skye watching him.

His heart jackhammered in his chest at the sight of her. Dressed in a cool, cotton sundress, wearing no makeup and with her eyes red-rimmed and swollen, she brought a sharp reminder of the pain he'd caused. Early this morning, before dawn, he'd given serious consideration to slipping out of the house unseen by Skye. But he couldn't bring himself to do anything quite so cowardly.

Now, he was glad he hadn't, even if it was just to see her beautiful face one last time.

Tyler drew in a deep breath. He'd gotten himself into this mess. Come hell or high water, he was going to see himself through it.

"I told you I've been hanging around here too long," he said, grinning wryly. "You're starting to pick up my bad habits...like sneaking up on a person."

She almost smiled. "Did you get your clothes out of the laundry? I had to wash a few things yesterday. I thought I might as well throw some of yours in, too."

He nodded. "I got 'em. Thank you."

Silence strained between them.

He glanced around the bedroom that had been his home for the past few weeks, taking in the rocking chair, the pinewood bed and the old-fashioned quilt he'd carefully smoothed back in place only moments ago. He knew he was going to miss this room...this house that had felt like home.

Tyler closed his duffel bag, the zipper making a loud rasping noise in the quiet room. He swore that if he listened hard enough, he could almost hear the sound of the seconds hand ticking by on his watch. The silence unnerved him. The atmosphere was entirely too serious. He wished he could figure out a way to lighten things up, to smooth over his departure.

Picking up the duffel bag and slinging it over his shoulder, he turned to the door...and to Skye. "I guess it's time for me to go."

She gave a quick nod, then stepped aside, giving him plenty of leeway to maneuver. The message was clear. She didn't want him touching her.

After last night, and the intimacies they'd almost shared, her attitude seemed a tad ironic. About as useful as closing the barn door after the cows have already escaped. Either way, it was too little, too late.

Tyler settled his black cowboy hat on his head and strode down the hall, not looking back to see if she followed. He stepped outside the coolness of the house and into the heat of the midday sunlight. Sweat beaded his skin, making his shirt cling to his back. His truck didn't have air-conditioning. It was going to be one helluva trip back to town. Opening the driver's side door, he tossed the duffel bag inside and hazarded a glance behind him.

To his relief, Skye was still with him. Stopping a few feet away from the pickup, she studied him, her big, blue eyes wide and uncertain.

Silently, Tyler chastised himself for all the trouble he'd caused her. "I guess this is where I say goodbye."

Polite as ever, she straightened her shoulders and dutifully said, "Goodbye, Tyler. It's been…interesting."

"Hell, Skye, no need to sugarcoat it." He shook his head, giving a short, humorless laugh. "It's been a lousy visit all the way around. I've made a real mess of your summer, haven't I?"

She bit her lip, not allowing herself to answer.

"I'm sorry, Skye…about last night, about everything."

"There's nothing to be sorry about." She said the words crisply, quickly. She averted her gaze, making it clear she didn't want to discuss the events that had transpired between them.

He respected her wishes. Struggling to find the right words, he steered the subject to safer ground. Softly, he said, "I owe you, Skye. You took me in when no one else would."

"You don't owe me a thing, Tyler," she said, meeting his gaze once again. "Helping each other…that's what friends are for."

"Some friend, huh?" He took off his cowboy hat and raked his fingers through his hair, giving the ranch a final inspection. Not that he'd admit as much to anyone else, but he was going to miss this ol' place. Even if the house and barn could use a coat of paint, and the fences were in need of mending, and the grass shouted to be mowed, it still felt like home. It sure as hell beat traveling to a different town every other night of the week. "Well, Skye, good luck with that thesis of yours. I hope you'll be happy with Ralph in Boston. If you're ever back in Texas, look me up sometime."

"Sure, Tyler." As brittle as it might be, for the first time that morning, she smiled. "I'll just look for you at the nearest rodeo."

The reminder of his uncertain career caught him by

surprise, taking his breath away. He hid his unease by putting on his cowboy hat, pulling it low over his brow, giving himself time to regain his composure. "Right. Well, goodbye, Skye."

"Bye, Tyler. Be careful on those bulls."

He forced a grin. "Yeah, I'll remember."

Saying nothing further, he climbed into the truck, slamming the door behind him. Skye stepped back as he gunned the motor to life. Tipping his hat, he shifted the truck into gear and headed for town.

Skye remained standing on the driveway, watching him until she was just a tiny speck in his rearview mirror. He'd thought getting kicked around by a two-thousand-pound bull was the hardest thing he'd ever done.

It didn't even compare to telling Skye goodbye.

The truck bounced over the ruts and potholes of the dirt road. Each jolt brought a dull ache low in his back, reminding him of the doctor's warning. As much as he'd like to deny it, his body would never be the same. He would never ride a bull again, not without risking permanent injury to his spine.

The ranch faded into the horizon as he pulled the truck onto the black-topped highway. He put the pedal to the metal and picked up speed, feeling as though he couldn't go fast enough, knowing all the while he was only running away.

Running away from the fact that he'd lied to Skye.

He wasn't the man she thought him to be. He never would be a champion bull rider ever again. He was a man without a future.

What could he offer a woman like Skye, who deserved so much more?

A squat, wooden building with a tin roof and a faded beer sign out front appeared before him on the side of the road. He licked his lips, feeling suddenly parched. Not giving himself a chance to reconsider, he veered the truck off the road, kicking up a cloud of dust as he braked to a stop in front of the tavern.

He popped open the truck's door and stepped outside into the hot, dusty sunshine. His boots thudded against the wooden porch as he strode to the tavern's entrance. Darkness met him at the door as he stepped inside. He waited, giving his eyes a moment to readjust before heading for the bar.

A noisy game of pool was being played in the corner. Two cowboys in a booth looked up from their drinks, eyeing him curiously, before returning their attention to more important matters. A blond-haired woman sitting at the bar, wearing a pair of too-tight jeans and a snug-fitting halter top, set her sights on him. He ignored the come-hither glance she sent his way and took his place on the opposite side of the bar.

Hooking the heels of his boots on the rung of a bar stool, he sat down and waited to be served.

The bartender, an older man with gray hair and tired blue eyes, sidled over to join him. "What's it going to be?"

"Whiskey, with a beer chaser," Tyler said, his tone curt, inviting no further conversation.

The bartender nodded and moved away. Moments later, he returned, placing a shot glass of whiskey and a foaming mug of beer before him. Tyler reached in his pocket for his money and peeled off enough bills to pay the man for his trouble.

Alone once again, he stared at the amber liquid. It had been years since he'd last had a drink. Some of the hardest years of his life. Then, he had a reason to stay sober. He was somebody. He was a champion.

Now, he had no career.

No Skye.

No life.

What was keeping him from getting stinking drunk?

The glass blurred and a picture of Skye formed in his mind's eye. Skye with her dark curling hair, her petite curves, and her sweet smile. He could almost see her looking up at him with those big blue eyes of hers, so innocent and trusting.

Though God knew, he didn't deserve her trust. He'd proven that much last night.

He'd lied to her from the get-go.

She thought he was some kind of hero.

He picked up the shot glass, rolling it back and forth between his hands, watching as the liquid nearly tipped out along the sides. Skye didn't know what kind of fool he really was…just how little courage he really had.

He didn't deserve her.

But that didn't stop him from wanting her.

Slowly, he lowered the glass to the smooth surface of the bar top, pushing it away. Even though Skye wasn't going to be a part of his life, he knew he couldn't allow himself to do anything that would disappoint her.

Ignoring the curious stares of the bar's customers, Tyler strode from the tavern, leaving the whiskey and the beer untouched.

Chapter Ten

The phone rang nearly ten times before her mind registered the insistent peal. Feeling as though her arms were encased in lead, Skye picked up the receiver. Somehow she managed a weary, "Hello."

"Skye?"

She winced at the concern in her father's voice. "Gus, how are yo—"

"What's the matter?" he demanded, ignoring the usual salutations.

"Nothing," she insisted, rolling her eyes. "I'm just tired. I was up half the night finishing my thesis."

"So you're done."

"That's right. Signed, sealed and ready to be delivered." She gave a weak-sounding laugh. "I was beginning to think I'd never finish that paper."

"I knew you would," he said, his voice gruff with paternal pride. "You're still planning on leaving then?"

"Yep, first thing in the morning. I've already got my bags packed." She glanced at the stack of bedsheets in her hand, which she was in the process of using to cover the sofas and chairs. In the six weeks since Tyler had left, the house had been as quiet as a tomb. Now it was beginning to resemble one. "I was just starting to get things ready to close up the house."

"Well, that can wait. Get yourself fancied up. I'm taking you out for dinner."

"Dinner?"

"That's right. I'm not letting my little girl leave without a night on the town to say goodbye."

"Gus, it's a long trip back to school," she said, searching her mind for a valid excuse. "I was planning to make it an early night...get to bed, get some sleep. I'm not really up for a party."

"Are you that anxious to get back to your Ralph?"

Skye winced at the mention of Ralph's name. Her engagement to Ralph, as short-lived as it was, was over. Last night, they'd talked openly and honestly, and they decided they would be better off if they parted ways, releasing each other to find true and lasting happiness.

Not that she had any intention of telling Gus of her breakup with Ralph. Her father would never let her leave Texas if he knew the truth.

"Ralph has nothing to do with it," she said finally. "It's just time for me to go."

"Well, I'm not taking no for an answer," he said in a determined voice that brooked no arguments. "You've been holing up in that house, working all summer. What kind of vacation is that to remember Texas by?"

She smiled despite herself, imagining the scowl on her daddy's face. "You're not going to give up until I say yes, are you, Gus?"

"You've got that right."

"Then I guess I don't have a choice," she said, laughing. The amusement faded, as a discomfiting thought worked its way into her mind. She shifted uncomfortably. "I'll go to dinner with you, Gus, on one condition."

"What's that?"

"That it's just you and me…no one else."

"Now, honey, the boys were hopin'—"

"No one else, Gus," she said in an equally determined voice. When it came to push or shove, she was her daddy's girl, after all…stubborn. "Or I'm staying home."

Gus hesitated, then said, "Sure, honey, whatever you want. The boys will just have to wait for another day to spend time with my little girl."

The tension melted from her muscles. At least she wouldn't have to suffer the embarrassment of facing Tyler again. "Shall I meet you at the store?"

"Naw, I'll come get ya. Slim said he'd close up for me tonight. I'll be there in a couple of hours."

Skye returned the receiver to its cradle. Clutching the sheets in her arms, she sat down hard in a nearby chair, her legs feeling shaky, unable to hold her weight. She looked around the house that had belonged to her grandmother and felt the tears sting her eyes. Her vision blurred. This was her last night in the house where so many memories had been made. Memories of her turbulent childhood, her defiant teenage years, and now of a bittersweet love affair of her adulthood.

She wouldn't be able to come back to this house without remembering Tyler, and what might have been. He was her first, and her greatest love. His mere touch had set her on fire, like no other man's possibly could. It would be a long time before she forgot him…if ever.

Tyler would always have a special place in her heart.

Skye whisked the tears from her eyes, as well as the disturbing memories from her mind, refusing to let her thoughts become maudlin. She'd wasted enough tears over Tyler Bradshaw. It was time to move on, put the past where it belonged, firmly behind her.

With that encouraging thought, she stood, dropping the bedsheets onto the empty dining room table. Gus had said, *Get yourself fancied up*. Well, that was just what she was going to do. A night on the town was beginning to sound like the cure for what ailed her.

Three hours later, wearing her best, sleeveless black dress and a pair of strappy gold sandals with three-inch heels, she sat across the table from her father and wished she'd tried harder to find an excuse to stay home.

The fancy clothes hadn't lifted her spirits as she'd hoped. In fact, she'd felt more than a little overdressed for the Tex-Mex restaurant that Gus had brought her to, where most of the customers wore blue jeans, cowboy shirts and boots.

"Eat up, honey. This restaurant's got the guaranteed best steaks in town," Gus said, nudging her attention toward her plate.

Skye looked at the two-inch-thick steak that took up the better part of a platter-size dish and sighed. The baked potato and accompanying side order of barbecued beans needed a separate plate to accommodate the meal. She didn't know why she'd allowed Gus to talk her into such a monstrosity of a dinner. It would be a miracle if she'd finish even a fourth of it.

"Come on, honey, eat something. You're looking too thin. How much weight have you lost this summer?"

Her father was the last person she needed to hear a lecture from on how to take care of herself. She picked up her knife and fork and cut off a piece of the tender steak. Medium well, just the way she liked it. Too bad she'd left her appetite at home. Too bad she hadn't stayed there with it.

"I don't know who's in a worse mood lately, you or Tyler. Trying to talk to either one of you is like trying to tiptoe through a minefield." Gus blew out a disgusted breath. "Either way, I have to watch my step."

"Tyler?" Slowly, she lowered her fork and stared at her father. "What's the matter with Tyler?"

"Nothing a good kick in the pants wouldn't take care of," Gus muttered, more to himself than to her.

Skye's eyes widened in surprise, not sure she'd ever heard him use such disparaging words when talking about his protégé. "What's Tyler done to you now, Gus?"

"It ain't what he's done to me." He gave a defeated sigh. "It's what he's going to do to himself."

A chill swept her body. She blamed the shivers on the air-conditioning blasting through the overhead vents. It couldn't be concern for Tyler. He was in her past for good, wasn't he?

"What are you talking about, Gus?" she asked, unable to stop her voice from trembling with unwanted emotion.

Gus frowned, looking at her warily. He shifted uncomfortably in his chair. "It's nothing...I shouldn't have said anything."

"Well, it's too late now. So you'd just better keep talking."

The unspoken threat in her tone did not go unnoticed by her father. Shaking his head, he muttered, "Tyler's going to have my hide. I promised him I wouldn't say anything to you."

"Gus—"

"All right, all right..." He tossed his napkin on the table. "Lord, but the two of you are feisty tonight."

"Gus, please—"

He sighed. "Okay, I'll tell ya. There's a rodeo tonight over in Mesquite."

A fist of fear tightened her heart. "So?"

"So, Tyler's planning on riding."

"No..." The word left her mouth on a ragged breath of denial. She swallowed hard, feeling her father's curious gaze, knowing her reaction went beyond that of the concern of a mere friend. "It's only been a couple of months since he hurt himself. Surely he's not ready for that sort of strain on his back."

"His back's not ever going to be ready for that sort of a strain," Gus said, snorting his disapproval. Then realizing what he'd just said, he gave a sheepish grin. "Forget I said that."

She sat back in her chair and crossed her arms, sending him what she hoped was her most threatening look. "No way, Gus. You're the one who started this—you're going to finish it now. Tell me exactly what you meant."

Slowly, the words tumbled from Gus's lips. He told her everything, from the back injury, to the doctor's warning, to Tyler's inability to accept his fate. When he admitted that Tyler might not walk away from another injury to his spine, Skye was on her feet in a burst of unfettered anger.

"What time is Tyler supposed to be riding?" she demanded.

Gus glanced at his watch. "Not for another hour or so."

"Good," she said, her words crisp, cool, belying the turmoil boiling inside her. "You've got a half an hour to get me to that rodeo."

Gus hesitated, looking uncertain whether or not to listen to her demands.

"Now, Gus." She grabbed his arm, yanking him to his feet. "If you think I'm going to let Tyler ruin his life, you're crazier than he is. For once in your life, don't just sit back and let things happen. Take a stand, show you care.''

Gus looked taken aback by the vehemence behind her words. "Skye, sweetheart...you know I care.''

Now wasn't the time for a heart-to-heart talk with her father. She'd let Tyler slip through her fingers once before. She wasn't going to make that mistake again. Time was a-wasting. Tyler's life, her life, depended upon her getting to him as fast as she could. "I know you do, Gus. I just need your help here, okay?''

"Sure, honey, whatever you want." He tossed a handful of bills on the table to pay for their untouched meal. Grabbing her arm, he led her toward the exit. "After we talk some sense into Tyler's thick skull, you and me, we're going to have ourselves a long talk. Starting with...exactly what's been going on between you and Tyler this summer.''

She heard the determined tone in her father's voice. She glanced at the firm set of his jaw and knew she wouldn't be able to explain away her actions easily. This time, it was her turn to sigh.

"Don't do this, Tyler," Joey said, his voice a low plea. "It's too late to get your spot back in the standings. You've got nothing more to prove and everything to lose by riding that bull.''

Tyler stared unseeingly at the bull in the holding pen. Slamming its bulky body into the rails, kicking up sawdust and dirt beneath its hooves, snorting its displeasure, the bull looked as uneasy as Tyler felt. It was as though he, too, sensed the importance of this night.

His friend couldn't be more wrong—Tyler had everything to prove with this ride. One way or another, tonight would be his last time on the back of a bull. He could not—would not—walk away from bull riding with his tail between his legs.

If his career was at an end, it would end with a fight.

Not a whimper of defeat.

His pride was all he had left to hold on to. He wouldn't give it up easily.

The noise of the rodeo pressed in around him. The announcer called out the results of the bareback rides. A roar of approval arose in the stands. That glorious roar of approval. How many times had he been busted up by a bull just to hear those fleeting shouts of glory?

Too many times to count, he reminded himself, shaking his head.

"Tyler, are you listening to me?" Joey demanded.

"I heard you," Tyler said, his tone clipped, dismissive.

Slim, Bucky, Mark and the rest of the boys shifted restlessly around them, sensing trouble in the air.

The announcement for the bull riders could be heard overhead. An odd quivering sensation fluttered in the pit of his stomach. Ignoring the warning signs, Tyler pushed himself from the fence, making his way to the chutes.

Joey stepped in front of him, using his massive body as a formidable roadblock.

Tyler stared him down, his gaze hard, unwavering. "You don't want to do this, my friend."

"Neither do you," Joey said, his voice deceivingly soft and gentle. "If you're not going to listen to reason, then maybe you'll listen to the sound of my fist in your ear."

Slim cleared his throat. "Tyler…Joey, now isn't the time—"

Joey silenced him with a single, sharp glance.

Slim stepped back, giving the pair plenty of room.

"What's it going to be, Tyler?" Joey asked.

Instinctively, Tyler balled his fists at his sides. He shored up his stance, locking his knees, stiffening his muscles. Like a tightly coiled spring, he was ready to pounce at a moment's notice.

Until he heard a familiar voice call out to him. A voice so unexpected, he had to look twice to believe it was really her. With Gus following closely behind, Skye was running toward him.

Dressed in a sexy black dress, wobbling on a pair of ankle-spraining high heels, she looked out of place among the boisterous group of rodeo regulars. She looked like a pretty little flower among a patch of wild, straggly weeds.

"Skye—"

"Don't you Skye me, Tyler Bradshaw," she hollered as she marched up to him and jabbed a finger at his chest, a furious glint in her eyes. Tyler swallowed hard at the lump of unease in his throat. Joey's anger was starting to look harmless in comparison to Skye's fury. "Tell me you're not getting on that bull."

Scowling, Tyler sought and found his old friend's gaze. Gus shrugged his wide shoulders and faded back a step or two, staying out of the line of fire.

"Now listen to me, Skye," Tyler said, keeping his voice low, vainly trying to keep their conversation private. He failed miserably. The boys leaned closer, craning their necks to get a better view of the unexpected show. "This doesn't have anything to do with you."

"Nothing to do with me?" she sputtered. Her blue eyes flashed with indignation. "It has everything to do with me."

"Skye, this isn't the time—"

"When do you suggest we have this conversation, Tyler? When you're in the hospital, too broken-up to walk?" Oblivious to the interest they were gathering from nearby spectators, she continued, her next words coming out of left field, taking him by surprise. "I'm in love with you, you thick-headed cowboy. I'll be damned if I'm going to let you hurt yourself anymore."

Tyler ignored the round of catcalls from his friends. He kept his gaze fixed upon her face. "What did you say?"

She rolled her eyes, giving him an impatient shake of her head. "What's the matter with you, Tyler? Those bulls drop you on your head too many times? Can't you hear?" Loud enough for half the arena to hear her, she repeated her earlier proclamation. "I said I love you. If you won't quit riding the bulls for me, then do it for our baby."

"Baby?" A deep voice boomed in the background, stealing the word straight from Tyler's mouth.

Before he could utter a protest in his own defense, Tyler felt a strong hand on his shoulder. Just before he was whirled around to face the condemnation of Skye's daddy. He saw the anger in his old friend's face. Saw the fist being raised before he could stop it from happening. Like a slow-motion picture, everything else blurred around him. Time stood still as he watched, then felt the well-placed right to his jaw.

The force of the blow sent him reeling backward. He hit the fence of the holding pen with a clatter of noise and confusion. Sliding downward to the ground, all hell broke loose as pain splintered his numbed senses.

"Daddy, no," Skye screamed. "His back, Gus. Don't hurt his back."

Tyler shook the starburst of light from his head, reaching for a rung of the fence, trying to pull himself to his feet.

Unmindful of her pretty dress and silk stockings, Skye knelt down beside him, pushing him back onto the ground. "Are you crazy?" she whispered. "He's going to kill you if you try to get up again."

Tyler blinked at the fuzzy effects of pain. He stared at her, feeling confused. Spitting out blood, he asked, "What baby, Skye?"

"Ours, silly," she said, giving him a wink and a conspiratorial grin. "The one of many that I plan to have with you..." she shot a withering glance at her father "...someday soon."

"You mean you're not pregnant?" Gus asked, rubbing his bruised knuckles with his uninjured hand.

"Of course not," Skye said, raising her nose in haughty indignation. "Tyler's too much of a gentleman to allow something like that to happen."

Tyler ignored the snickers of amusement from the cowboys standing nearby.

"Now, just what is that supposed to mean?" Gus took another threatening step toward him.

Tyler held up his hands in surrender. "It means I don't want to fight my future father-in-law."

"Father-in-law?" Gus's scowl relaxed only slightly. "Does this mean you're planning on marryin' my daughter?"

"If she'll have me," Tyler admitted. He looked at Skye, holding his breath, as he searched her sweet face for an answer.

The rowdy group of cowboys surrounding them went unnaturally still.

It seemed as though the entire arena was waiting for Skye's answer.

Her brow wrinkled into a frown. She shot him a stern look and demanded, "Are you still planning on riding that bull?"

"No, ma'am," he said, shaking his head. "I've had enough shocks to my system for one night, thank you."

"Then I'll marry you," she said.

A cheer of approval arose from the crowd.

Tyler grinned at the irony. He had wanted one last roar of approval from the crowd before he called an end to his career. Well, he'd gotten his eight seconds of glory, and then some. All he'd had to do to earn it was lose his heart.

"I love you, Skye," he said, ignoring the cowboys standing nearby, listening without discretion to each and every word he spoke.

"I love you too, Tyler." She wrapped her arms around his neck and fell into his arms, getting dirt and sawdust all over her pretty dress.

Tyler cried out as she grazed his sore jaw.

"Sorry...I'm so sorry," she said, laughing, and not looking a bit contrite in his opinion.

Tyler shook his head. "Skye, with you in my life, I'm not going to need to ride another bull again. You're more trouble than this man can handle."

Her eyes misted, she looked ridiculously close to tears. "Tyler, that's the nicest thing you've ever said to me."

"I promise you, Skye. It won't be the last."

With that he pulled her into his arms, ignoring the ache in his jaw, and kissed her.

Epilogue

One year later

"What do you think's taking them so long?" Tyler asked, squinting through the ranch's kitchen window, peering down the dusty lane which led to town.

"I don't know, Tyler," Skye said, careful to keep any sign of impatience from her voice. "You don't think it's because they're not due to arrive for...oh, say, another hour?"

Tyler turned from the window, his hands on his hips, and frowned. "Another hour?"

"Uh-huh," she said, sipping her herbal tea, hiding an amused smile behind the rim of her mug. "I tried to tell you before, when you insisted on getting up at the crack of dawn, that we had plenty of time for *other* things."

A devilish grin replaced his frown. "What other things, Skye?"

"Why sleep, of course," she said, unable to stop the heat from flushing her body.

"Sounds kind of boring. Not nearly enough fun to keep my mind off of my troubles." His grin deepened. He took a step closer. "What else did you have in mind?"

She set the mug of herbal tea down on the counter, out of harm's way, and studied her nails, affecting a disinterest she didn't really feel. "Nothing I'd care to share with you now. You had your chance earlier, but you pooh-poohed away your opportunity."

"Dang, it was going to be that good, huh?"

"Not that you'll ever know," she said, raising her chin and tightening the belt of her bathrobe.

"I wouldn't bet on that," he drawled, closing the gap between them.

"Tyler Bradshaw, you are the most ornery, bull-headed man—"

He quieted her protests with a kiss. By the time he'd finished, she felt breathless and dizzy. Even after a year of marriage, he still had that effect over her. He gave her a satisfied grin. "I may be ornery, but you're the one who married me. So what does that have to say about your self?"

She shrugged her shoulders. "That I'm a glutton for punishment?"

"You're a glutton, all right," he said, chuckling. "But what you've got an appetite for, I'm more than willing to supply."

"Tyler," she said, giving a shocked expression. "I never—"

"Never? Now, Skye, you know you can't lie to me." He traced a finger across her lower lip, sending a tingling sensation racing through her body. Skye shivered with delight. "I'm the one with the bags under his eyes, proof of all those sleepless nights I've had to spend taking care of your…hunger cravings."

"If I have any cravings, it's all your fault." She placed a protective hand on her burgeoning tummy. "You're the one who got me in this condition."

Tyler shook his head and smiled. "That's right, blame the father for everything that goes wrong."

She raised her chin in mock indignation. "Funny, I never heard you complain before."

"And I'm not complaining now," he growled.

Before she could protest, he lifted her off the floor, setting her on the counter in front of him, putting her at a more advantageous position. She gasped when he slid his work-roughened fingers up the length of her smooth legs and parted her thighs. He slipped in between and pressed his lean body snug against her, showing her just how few complaints he really had.

"Tyler, I was only teasing when I said we had plenty of time."

"I know, I know," he murmured, nibbling on her neck. His hand sought and found the round curve of her breast. "An hour isn't nearly enough time. But I promise, Skye, I'll make it up to you tonight."

"Jack's truck is already in the lot," she protested, as she fumbled with the snaps on his cowboy shirt. "What if he decides to help himself to a cup of coffee and walks in to find us?"

He loosened the knot of her bathrobe, slipping his hands inside. "Jack knows better than to roust a couple of honeymooners out of bed."

"But we're not in bed, are we?"

The last snap gave way with a loud pop in her hand. She sighed as Tyler's shirt fell open, giving her an intimate view of his well-muscled chest. It seemed hard to believe that almost a year ago Tyler had been incapacitated in any way. While he still had to be careful with his back, he was more than capable of performing most normal activities…thank goodness.

Tyler slid his hand downward to cover the slight swell of her tummy. "Is Tyler Jr. still sleeping?"

"If he is, he won't be for long." Skye smiled. At five months, she no longer suffered the ill effects of morning sickness. In fact, she found the second trimester of her pregnancy to be most interesting. Not only had her appetite returned, but she'd become insatiable in other ways…as Tyler had so ungraciously pointed out.

She brought a hand to his belt buckle…and nearly cried out in disappointment when she heard the thunder of an approaching semitruck. "They're early."

"Damn. Their timing could have been better," Tyler muttered, a regretful look crossing his face. He kissed her hard on the mouth, sending her senses into overload. Then he gently lowered her from the counter, setting her back down on her feet. She clung to him until the room stopped spinning. Chuckling, he said, "Keep that thought. We'll take up where we left off tonight, when we've got more time."

"I'm holding you to that, cowboy."

Snapping the buttons of his shirt closed, he reached for his hat, settling it over his sunbleached blond hair, and grinned. "That's one promise I won't mind keeping."

Tucking in his shirttails, he turned to leave.

"Tyler," she said on a breathless note. Unease caught in her throat, making it hard to breathe.

He turned, frowning slightly.

Nervously, she looked outside through the window at the flurry of activity taking place in the yard of her grandmother's ranch. Under Jack's direction, not one, but two large truckloads of rodeo animals were being unloaded and corraled into waiting pens.

Tyler had worked hard this past year, turning this run-down ranch into a working, thriving enterprise. With Gus's blessing, he'd pooled his rodeo winnings into stocking the farm with thoroughbred horses. They now owned one of the fastest growing breeding ranches on this side of Texas.

When he'd confided his dream of opening up an annual workshop for wannabe rodeo riders, she'd been hesitant in giving her approval. The temptation to ride again would be immense. She couldn't help but wonder if he'd have the strength to stay off the bulls.

Admitting her fears, however, would be the same as saying she didn't trust him.

Tyler was watching her, his expression curious.

Skye forced a smile. "Aren't you forgetting something?"

He frowned, looking confused.

"A kiss for luck," she said, stepping up to him, ignoring the butterflies dancing in her stomach. "Remember?"

His easy grin returned. "How could I forget?"

Obligingly, she lifted her lips to his. The kiss, while sweet and tender, ended too soon.

At her sigh of discontent, he whispered, "Don't worry, Skye, I promise I won't go near the bulls."

She dropped her gaze, fidgeting with the lapels of his shirt, unwilling to let him see the concern in her eyes.

"I've got too many reasons to stay in one piece…you, and the baby." He covered her hands with his, prying her fingers from his shirt collar. He turned them over, placing a tender kiss on each of her palms. "Don't you know? I'm too damned happy to risk everything I've got on eight seconds of glory."

She looked up into his eyes and saw the sincerity reflected in them. The tension slowly melted from her body.

"Now as much as I like seeing you in a bathrobe and nothing else, I've got about a dozen cowboys on their way to help out for the day. It might be a good idea if you changed before they arrived. I'd hate to have to beat them up for ogling, seeing how they're helping us out and all."

"Good idea," she said, unable to stop the goofy grin from forming.

He hesitated. "You're still planning on staying for the day, aren't you?"

"I wouldn't miss it for the world," she said, reaching up to tuck a stray strand of blond hair beneath his hat. "I've told them at the Junior College, I'd be taking the day off to help my husband. Besides, I'll just be missing a couple of faculty meetings. Classes don't start until next week."

"Lord," he said, shaking his head. "I still can't believe I'm married to a college professor."

"I can't believe I married a cowboy."

He raised a brow. "Any regrets?"

"Not yet." She couldn't help but laugh at the scowl forming on his face. Quickly, she amended her answer. "Not ever, Tyler. You're one cowboy I'm glad I married."

*　*　*　*　*

If you enjoyed what you just read,
then we've got an offer you can't resist!

Take 2 bestselling love stories FREE!

Plus get a FREE surprise gift!

Clip this page and mail it to Silhouette Reader Service™

IN U.S.A.
3010 Walden Ave.
P.O. Box 1867
Buffalo, N.Y. 14240-1867

IN CANADA
P.O. Box 609
Fort Erie, Ontario
L2A 5X3

YES! Please send me 2 free Silhouette Romance® novels and my free surprise gift. Then send me 6 brand-new novels every month, which I will receive months before they're available in stores. In the U.S.A., bill me at the bargain price of $2.90 plus 25¢ delivery per book and applicable sales tax, if any*. In Canada, bill me at the bargain price of $3.25 plus 25¢ delivery per book and applicable taxes**. That's the complete price and a savings of over 10% off the cover prices—what a great deal! I understand that accepting the 2 free books and gift places me under no obligation ever to buy any books. I can always return a shipment and cancel at any time. Even if I never buy another book from Silhouette, the 2 free books and gift are mine to keep forever. So why not take us up on our invitation. You'll be glad you did!

215 SEN CNE7
315 SEN CNE9

Name	(PLEASE PRINT)	
Address	Apt.#	
City	State/Prov.	Zip/Postal Code

* Terms and prices subject to change without notice. Sales tax applicable in N.Y.
** Canadian residents will be charged applicable provincial taxes and GST.
  All orders subject to approval. Offer limited to one per household.
® are registered trademarks of Harlequin Enterprises Limited.

SROM99   ©1998 Harlequin Enterprises Limited

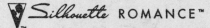

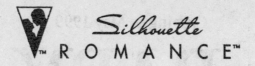

COMING NEXT MONTH